WHISPERS IN THE DARK
A BOOK OF SPOOKS

RUSKIN BOND

Illustrations by Bombay Design House

PUFFIN BOOKS

PUFFIN BOOKS

USA | Canada | UK | Ireland | Australia
New Zealand | India | South Africa | China

Puffin Books is part of the Penguin Random House group of companies
whose addresses can be found at global.penguinrandomhouse.com

Published by Penguin Random House India Pvt. Ltd
7th Floor, Infinity Tower C, DLF Cyber City,
Gurgaon 122 002, Haryana, India

First published in Puffin Books by Penguin Random House India 2016

ISBN 9780143333593

Typeset in Baskerville by Manipal Digital Systems, Manipal
Printed at Thomson Press India Ltd, New Delhi

CONTENTS

INTRODUCTION

H ello, Mr Bond! It's jolly nice of you to invite me to write the introduction to this nutty collection of spooky stories that you've written over the years.

I've been trying to contact you for some time but it seems you aren't really very psychic. I wave out to you but you don't notice me. I walk right into you but you don't see or feel me. But we were friends once, in our golden schooldays. And our friendship would have gone on, beyond school and college, if someone hadn't come up from behind and pushed me into the swimming pool.

Had you been around, you would have jumped in to save me from drowning, knowing I couldn't swim. But I was on my own that afternoon, actually looking for you. Until some devil came up from behind—and pushed!

Over the years I had my suspicions, and I knew that if ever I came face-to-face with the fellow, he'd see me and simply die of fright.

Well, it happened last year at the school reunion. I'm sorry you weren't there; it would have been fun—especially when old Ranjit, now a minister, got up on the rostrum and made one of his long, uninspiring speeches. I was there in my spirit form, of course, but he saw me and recognized me the minute I materialized in front of him. He clutched at his heart, let out a strangled cry, stepped back and tumbled off the rostrum— dead of a heart attack. It's a bit like drowning, I'm told.

Well, old boy, I won't hang around any more. I've had my little bit of revenge. And now it's time to move on and see what lies on the other side of the curtain.

Thanks again for letting me go through your stories. Some of them aren't too bad.

Good luck, old soul, and may the book sell a million.

Your old pal,
Sammy M. Spiritland

OUT OF THE DARK

At a ruin upon a hill outside the town,
I found some shelter from a summer storm.
An alcove in a wall, moss-green and redolent of bats,
But refuge from the wind and rain; and entrance once
To what had been a home, a mansion large and spacious;
Now dream-wrecked, desolate.
And as I stood there, pondering
Upon the mutability of stone, I thought I heard
A haunting cry, insistent on the wind—
'Oh son, please let me in,
Oh son, please let me in . . .'

Just the soughing of the wind
In the bending, keening pines;
Just the rain sibilant on old stones;
Or was it something more, a voice
Trapped in the woof of time, imploring still,
And lingering at some door which stood
Where now I sheltered on a barren hill.

At home, that night, I settled down
To read, the bed lamp on. The night was warm,
The storm had passed and all was still outside,
When something, someone, moved about, came tapping on
    the door.

'Who's there?' I called.
The tapping stopped. And then,
Entreating, came that voice again,
'Oh son, please let me in!'
'Who's there, who's there?' I cried,
And crossed the cold stone floor,
Paused for a moment, hand on catch,
Then opened wide the door.
Bright moonlight streamed across the sill
And crept along the stair;
I peered outside, to right and left:
Bright road returned my stare.

But long before the dawn, I heard
That tapping once again;
Not on the door this time, but nearer still—
Now rapping quickly on the windowpane.
I lay quite still and held my breath
And thought—surely it's the old oak tree,
Leaves gently tapping on the glass,
Or a moth, or some great beetle winging past.
But through the darkness, pressing in,
As though in me it sought its will,
As though in me it yet would dwell—
'Oh son, please let me in . . .
Oh son, please let me in!'

ON FAIRY HILL

Those little green lights that I used to see twinkling away on Pari Tibba—there had to be a scientific explanation for them. I was sure of that. After dark, we see or hear many things that seem mysterious and irrational. And then, by the clear light of day, we find that the magic and the mystery have an explanation, after all.

I saw those lights occasionally, late at night, when I walked home from the town to my little cottage at the edge of the forest. They moved too fast to be torches or lanterns carried by people. And as there were no roads on Pari Tibba, they could not have been cycle- or cart-lamps. Someone told me there was phosphorus in the rocks and that this probably accounted for the luminous glow emanating from the hillside late at night. Possibly, but I was not convinced.

My encounter with the little people happened by the light of day.

One morning early in April, purely on an impulse, I decided to climb to the top of Pari Tibba and look around for myself. It was springtime in the Himalayan foothills. The sap was rising—in the trees, in the grass, in the wild flowers, in my own veins. I took the path through the oak forest, down to the little stream at the foot of the hill, and then up the steep slope of Pari Tibba, Hill of Fairies.

It was quite a scramble to get to the top. The path ended at the stream at the bottom of the slope. I had to clutch at brambles and tufts of grass to make the ascent. Fallen pine needles, slippery underfoot, made it difficult to get a foothold. But finally I made it to the top—a grassy plateau fringed by pines and a few wild medlar trees now clothed in white blossom.

It was a pretty spot. And as I was hot and sweaty, I removed most of my clothing and lay down under a medlar to rest. The climb had been quite tiring. But a fresh breeze soon revived me. It made a soft humming sound in the pines. And the grass, sprinkled with yellow buttercups, buzzed with the sound of crickets and grasshoppers.

After some time, I stood up and surveyed the scene. To the north, Landour, with its rusty red-roofed cottages; to the south, the wide valley and a silver stream flowing towards the Ganga. To the west, were rolling hills, patches of forest and a small village tucked into a fold of the mountain.

Disturbed by my presence, a barking deer ran across the clearing and down the opposite slope. A band of long-tailed blue magpies rose from the oak trees, glided across the knoll and settled in another copse of oaks.

I was alone, alone with the wind and the sky. It had probably been months, possibly years, since any human had passed that way. The soft, lush grass looked most inviting. I lay down again on the sun-warmed sward. Pressed and bruised by my weight, the catmint and clover in the grass gave out a soft fragrance. A ladybird climbed up my leg and began to explore my body. A swarm of white butterflies fluttered around me.

I slept.

I have no idea how long I slept. When I awoke, it was to experience an unusual soothing sensation all over my limbs, as though they were being gently stroked with rose petals.

All lethargy gone, I opened my eyes to find a little girl—or was it a woman?—about two inches tall, sitting cross-legged on my chest and studying me intently. Her hair fell in long, black tresses. Her skin was the colour of honey. Her firm little breasts were like tiny acorns. She held a buttercup, which was larger than her hand, and she was stroking my skin with it.

I was tingling all over. A sensation of sensual joy surged through my limbs.

A tiny boy—man?—also naked, now joined the elfin girl, and they held hands and looked into my eyes, smiling. Their teeth were like little pearls, their lips, soft petals of apricot blossom. Were these the nature spirits, the flower fairies, I had often dreamt of?

I raised my head, and saw that there were scores of little people all over me. The delicate and gentle creatures were exploring my body with caressing gestures. Some of them were laving me with dew or pollen or some other soft essence. I closed my eyes again. Waves of pure physical pleasure swept over me. I had never known anything like it. It was endless, all-embracing. My limbs turned to water. The sky revolved around me, and I must have fainted.

When I came to, perhaps an hour later, the little people had gone. The fragrance of honeysuckle lingered in the air. A deep rumble overhead made me look up. Dark clouds had gathered, threatening to rain. Had the thunder frightened them away to their abode beneath the rocks and roots? Or had they simply tired of sporting with an unknown newcomer? Mischievous they were; for when I looked around for my clothes, I could not find them anywhere.

A wave of panic surged over me. I ran here and there, looking behind shrubs and tree trunks, but to no avail. My clothes had disappeared, along with the fairies—if indeed they were fairies!

It began to rain. Large drops cannoned off the dry rocks. Then it hailed, and soon the slope was covered with ice. There was no shelter. Naked, I clambered down as far as the stream. There was no one to see me—except for a wild mountain goat speeding away in the opposite direction. Gusts of wind slashed rain and hail across my face and body. Panting and shivering, I took shelter beneath an overhanging rock until the storm had passed. By then it was almost dusk, and I was able to ascend the path to my cottage without encountering anyone, apart from a band of startled langurs who chattered excitedly on seeing me.

I couldn't stop shivering, so went straight to bed. I slept a deep, dreamless sleep through the afternoon, evening and night, and woke up the next morning with a high fever.

Mechanically I dressed, made myself some breakfast and tried to get through the morning's chores. When I took my temperature, I found it was 104. So I swallowed a Brufen and went back to bed.

There I lay till late afternoon, when the postman's knocking woke me. I left my letters unopened on my desk—breaking a sacrosanct ritual—and returned to my bed.

The fever lasted almost a week and left me weak and feeble. I couldn't have climbed Pari Tibba again even if I'd wanted to. But I reclined on my window seat and looked at the clouds drifting over that bleak hill. Desolate it seemed, and yet strangely inhabited. When it grew dark, I waited for those little green fairy lights to appear; but these, it seemed, were now to be denied to me.

And so I returned to my desk, my typewriter, my newspaper articles and correspondence. It was a lonely period in my life. My marriage hadn't worked out: my wife, fond of high society and averse to living with an unsuccessful writer in a remote cottage in the woods, was pursuing her own, more successful career in Mumbai. I had always been rather half-hearted in my approach to making money, whereas she had always wanted more and more of it. She left me—left me with my books and my dreams . . .

Had it all been a dream, that strange episode on Pari Tibba? Had a too-active imagination conjured up those aerial spirits, those siddhas of the upper air? Or were they underground people, living deep within the bowels of the hill? If I was going to preserve my sanity, I knew I had better get on with the more mundane aspects of living—going into town to buy groceries, mending the leaking roof, paying the electricity bill, plodding up to the post office, and remembering to deposit the odd cheque that came my way. All the routine things that made life so dull and dreary.

The truth is, what we commonly call life is not really living at all. The regular and settled ways which we accept as the course of life are really the curse of life. They tie us down to the trivial and monotonous, and we will do almost anything to get away, ideally for a more exalted and fulfilling existence, but if that is not possible, for a few hours of forgetfulness in alcohol, drugs, forbidden sex or even golf. So it would give me great joy to go underground with the fairies. Those little people who have sought refuge in Mother Earth from mankind's killing ways are as vulnerable as butterflies and flowers. All things beautiful are easily destroyed.

I am sitting at my window in the gathering dark, penning these stray thoughts, when I see them coming—hand-in-hand, walking on a swirl of mist, suffused with all the radiant colours of the rainbow. For a rainbow has formed a bridge for them from Pari Tibba to the edge of my window.

I am ready to go with them to their secret lairs or to the upper air—far from the stifling confines of the world in which we toil . . .

Come, fairies, carry me away, to experience again the perfection I did that summer's day!

A DREADFUL GURGLE

Have you ever woken up in the night to find someone in your bed who wasn't supposed to be there?

Well, it happened to me when I was at a boarding school in Simla, many years ago.

I was sleeping in the senior dormitory, along with some twenty other boys, and my bed was positioned in a corner of the long room, at some distance from the others. There was no shortage of pranksters in our dormitory, and one had to look out for the introduction of stinging nettle, or pebbles, or possibly even a small lizard under the bed sheets. But I wasn't prepared for a body in my bed.

At first I thought a sleepwalker had mistakenly got into my bed, and I tried to push him out, muttering, 'Devinder, get back into your own bed. There isn't room for two of us.' Devinder was a notorious sleepwalker, who had even ended up on the roof on one occasion.

But it wasn't Devinder.

Devinder was a short boy, and this fellow was a tall, lanky person. His feet stuck out of the blankets at the foot of the bed.

It must be Ranjit, I thought. Ranjit had huge feet.

'Ranjit!' I hissed. 'Stop playing the fool, and get back to your own bed.'

No response.

I tried pushing, but without success. The body was heavy and inert. It was also very cold.

I lay there wondering who it could be, and then it began to dawn on me that the person beside me wasn't breathing. And I had the horrible realization that there was a corpse in my bed! How did it get there, and what was I to do about it?

'Vishal!' I called out to a boy who was sleeping a short distance away.

'Vishal, wake up, there's a corpse in my bed!'

Vishal did wake up. 'You're dreaming, Bond. Go to sleep and stop disturbing everyone.'

Just then, there was a groan, followed by a dreadful gurgle, from the body beside me. I shot out of bed, shouting at the top of my voice, waking up the entire dormitory.

Lights came on. There was total confusion. The housemaster came running. I told him, and everyone else, what had happened. They came to my bed and had a good look at it. But there was no one there.

On my insistence, I was moved to the other end of the dormitory. The house prefect, Johnson, took over my former bed.

Two nights passed without further excitement, and a couple of boys started calling me a funk and a scaredy-cat. My response was to punch one of them on the nose.

Then, on the third night, we were all woken by several ear-splitting shrieks, and Johnson came charging across the dormitory, screaming that two icy hands had taken him by the throat and tried to squeeze the life out of him. Lights came on, and the poor old housemaster came dashing in again. We calmed Johnson down and put him in a spare bed. The housemaster shone his torch on the boy's face and neck, and, sure enough, we saw several bruises on his flesh, and the outline of a large hand.

Next day, the offending bed was removed from the dormitory, but it was a few days before Johnson recovered from the shock. He was kept in the infirmary until the bruises disappeared, but for the rest of the year, he was a nervous wreck.

Our nursing sister, who had looked after the infirmary for many years, recalled that some twenty years earlier, a boy called Tomkins had died suddenly in the dormitory. He was very tall for his age and apparently suffered from a heart problem. That day, he had taken part in a football match, and had gone to bed looking pale and exhausted. Early next morning, when the bell rang for gym class, he was found stiff and cold, having apparently died during the night.

'He died peacefully, poor boy,' recalled our nursing sister.

But I'm not so sure. I can still hear that dreadful gurgle from the creature in my bed. And there was the struggle with Johnson. No, there was nothing peaceful about that death. Tomkins had gone most unwillingly . . .

A FACE IN THE DARK

Mr Oliver, an Anglo-Indian teacher, was returning to his school late one night, on the outskirts of the hill station of Simla. From before Kipling's time, the school had been run on the lines of English public schools, and the boys, most of them from wealthy Indian families, wore blazers, caps and ties. *Life* magazine, in a feature on India, had once called it the 'Eton of the East'. Oliver had been teaching in the school for several years.

The Simla Bazaar, with its cinemas and restaurants, was about three miles from the school, and Mr Oliver, a bachelor, usually strolled into the town in the evening, returning after dark, when he would take a shortcut through the pine forest.

When there was a strong wind, the pine trees made sad, eerie sounds that kept most people to the main road. But Mr Oliver was not a nervous or imaginative man. He carried a torch, and its gleam—the batteries were running down—moved fitfully down the narrow forest path. When its flickering light fell on the figure of a boy, who was sitting alone on a rock, Mr Oliver stopped. Boys were not supposed to be out after dark.

'What are you doing out here, boy?' asked Mr Oliver sharply, moving closer so that he could recognize the miscreant. But even as he approached the boy, Mr Oliver sensed that something was wrong. The boy appeared to be crying. His head hung down, he held his face in his hands, and his body shook convulsively. It was strange, soundless weeping, and Mr Oliver felt distinctly uneasy.

'Well, what's the matter?' He asked, his anger giving way to concern. 'What are you crying for?' The boy would not answer or look up. His body continued to be racked with silent sobbing. 'Come on, boy, you shouldn't be out here at this hour. Tell me the trouble. Look up!'

The boy looked up. He took his hands from his face and looked at his teacher. The light from Mr Oliver's torch fell on the boy's face—if you could call it a face.

It had no eyes, ears, nose or mouth. It was just a round, smooth head—with a school cap on top of it! And that's where the story should end. But for Mr Oliver, it did not end there.

The torch fell from his trembling hand. He turned and scrambled down the path, running blindly through the trees and calling for help. He was still running towards the school buildings when he saw a lantern swinging in the middle of the path. Mr Oliver stumbled up to the watchman, gasping for breath. 'What is it, sahib?' asked the watchman. 'Has there been an accident? Why are you running?'

'I saw something—something horrible—a boy weeping in the forest—and he had no face!'

'No face, sahib?'

'No eyes, nose, mouth—nothing!'

'Do you mean it was like this, sahib?' asked the watchman and raised the lamp to his own face. The watchman had no eyes, no ears, no features at all—not even an eyebrow! And that's when the wind blew the lamp out.

WHISPERING IN THE DARK

A wild night. Wind moaning, trees lashing themselves in a frenzy, rain beating down on the road, thunder over the mountains. Loneliness stretched ahead of me, a loneliness of the heart, as well as a physical loneliness. The world was blotted out by a mist that had come up from the valley, a thick, white, clammy shroud.

I groped through the forest, groped in my mind for the memory of a mountain path, some remembered rock or ancient deodar. Then a streak of blue lightning gave me a glimpse of a barren hillside and a house cradled in mist.

It was an old-world house, built of limestone, on the outskirts of a crumbling hill station. There was no light in its windows; the electricity had probably been disconnected long ago. But if I could get in, it would do for the night.

I had no torch, but at times the moon shone through the wild clouds, and trees loomed out of the mist like primeval giants. I reached the front door and found it locked from within. I walked round to the side and broke a windowpane, put my hand through shattered glass and found the bolt.

The window, warped by over a hundred monsoons, resisted at first. Then it yielded, and I climbed into the mustiness of a long-closed room, and the wind came in with me, scattering papers across the floor and knocking some unidentifiable object off a table. I closed the window, bolted it again; but the mist crawled through the broken glass, and the wind rattled it like a pair of castanets.

There were matches in my pocket. I struck three before a light flared up.

I was in a large room, crowded with furniture. Pictures on the walls. Vases on the mantelpiece. A candle stand. And, strangely enough, no cobwebs. For all its external look of neglect and dilapidation, the house had been cared for by someone. But before I could notice anything else, the match burnt out.

As I stepped further into the room, the old deodar flooring creaked beneath my weight. By the light of another match I reached the mantelpiece and lit the candle, noticing at the same time that the candlestick was a genuine antique with cut-glass hangings. A deserted cottage with good furniture and glass. I wondered why no one had ever broken in. And then realized that I had just done so.

I held the candlestick high and glanced round the room. The walls were hung with several watercolours and portraits in oils. There was no dust anywhere. But no one answered my call, no one responded to my hesitant knocking. It was as though the occupants of the house were in hiding, watching me obliquely from dark corners and chimneys.

I entered a bedroom and found myself facing a full-length mirror. My reflection stared back at me as though I were a stranger, as though my reflection belonged to the house, while I was only an outsider.

As I turned from the mirror, I thought I saw someone, something—some reflection other than mine—move behind me in the mirror. I caught a glimpse of whiteness, a pale oval face, burning eyes, long tresses, golden in the candlelight. But when I looked in the mirror again, there was nothing to be seen but my own pallid face.

A pool of water was forming at my feet. I set the candle down on a small table, found the edge of the bed—a large old four-poster—sat down, and removed my soggy shoes and socks. Then I took off my clothes and hung them over the back of a chair.

I stood naked in the darkness, shivering a little. There was no one to see me—and yet I felt oddly exposed, almost as though I had stripped in a room full of curious people.

I got under the bedclothes—they smelled slightly of eucalyptus and lavender—but found there was no pillow. That was odd. A perfectly made bed, but no pillow! I was too tired to hunt for one. So I blew out the candle—and the darkness closed in around me, and the whispering began . . .

The whispering began as soon as I closed my eyes. I couldn't tell where it came from. It was all around me, mingling with the sound of the wind coughing in the chimney, the stretching of old furniture, the weeping of trees outside in the rain.

Sometimes I could hear what was being said. The words came from a distance, a distance not so much of space as of time . . .

'Mine, mine, he is all mine . . .'

'He is ours, dear, ours.'

Whispers, echoes, words hovering around me with bats' wings, saying the most inconsequential things with a logical urgency.

'You're late for supper . . .'

'He lost his way in the mist.'

'Do you think he has any money?'

'To kill a turtle, you must first tie its legs to two posts.'

'We could tie him to the bed and pour boiling water down his throat.'

'No, it's simpler this way.'

I sat up. Most of the whispering had been distant, impersonal, but this last remark had sounded horribly near.

I relit the candle and the voices stopped. I got up and prowled around the room, vainly looking for some explanation for the voices. Once again, I found myself facing the mirror, staring at my own reflection, and the reflection of that other person, the girl with the golden hair and shining eyes. And this time she held a pillow in her hands. She was standing behind me.

I remembered then the stories I had heard as a boy, of two spinster sisters—one beautiful, one plain—who lured rich, elderly gentlemen into their boarding house and suffocated them in the night. The deaths had appeared quite natural, and they had got away with it for years. It was only the surviving sister's deathbed confession that had revealed the truth—and even then, no one had believed her.

But that had been many, many years ago, and the house had long since fallen down . . .

When I turned from the mirror, there was no one behind me. I looked again, and the reflection had gone.

I crawled back into the bed and put the candle out. And I slept and dreamt (or was I awake and did it really happen?) that the woman I had seen in the mirror stood beside the bed, leant over me, looked at me with eyes flecked with orange flames. I saw people moving in those eyes. I saw myself. And then her lips touched mine, lips so cold, so dry, that a shudder ran through my body.

And then, while her face became faceless and only the eyes remained, something else continued to press down upon me, something soft, heavy and shapeless, enclosing me in a suffocating embrace. I could not turn my head or open my mouth. I could not breathe.

I raised my hands and clutched feebly at the thing on top of me. And to my surprise it came away. It was only a pillow

that had somehow fallen over my face, half suffocating me, while I dreamt of a phantom kiss.

I flung the pillow aside. I flung the bedclothes from me. I had had enough whispering, of ownerless reflections, of pillows that fell on me in the dark. I would brave the storm outside rather than continue to seek rest in this tortured house.

I dressed quickly. The candle had almost guttered out. The house and everything in it belonged to the darkness of another time; I belonged to the light of day.

I was ready to leave. I avoided the tall mirror with its grotesque rococo design. Holding the candlestick before me, I moved cautiously into the front room. The pictures on the walls sprang to life.

One, in particular, held my attention, and I moved closer to examine it more carefully by the light of the dwindling candle. Was it just my imagination, or was the girl in the portrait the woman of my dream, the beautiful, pale reflection in the mirror? Had I gone back in time, or had time caught up with me?

I turned to leave, and the candle gave one final sputter and went out, plunging the room in darkness. I stood still for a moment, trying to collect my thoughts, to still the panic that came rushing upon me. Just then there was a knocking on the door.

'Who's there?' I called.

Silence. And then, again, the knocking, and this time a voice, low and insistent: 'Please let me in, please let me in . . .'

I stepped forward, unbolted the door and flung it open.

She stood outside, in the rain. Not the pale, beautiful one, but a wizened old hag with bloodless lips and flaring nostrils and—but where were the eyes? No eyes, no eyes!

She swept past me on the wind, and at the same time, I took advantage of the open doorway to run outside, to run gratefully into the pouring rain, to be lost for hours among the dripping trees, to be glad for all the leeches clinging to my flesh.

And when, with the dawn, I found my way at last, I rejoiced in birdsong and the sunlight piercing and scattering the clouds.

And today if you were to ask me if the old house is still there or not, I would not be able to tell you, for the simple reason that I haven't the slightest desire to go looking for it.

THE WIND ON HAUNTED HILL

Who–whoo–whooo, cried the wind as it swept down from the Himalayan snows.

It hurried over the hills and passes, and hummed and moaned in the tall pines and deodars.

On Haunted Hill there was little to stop the wind—only a few stunted trees and bushes, and the ruins of what had once been a small settlement.

On the slopes of the next hill there was a small village. People kept large stones on their tin roofs to prevent them from blowing away. There was nearly always a wind in these parts. Even on sunny days, doors and windows rattled, chimneys choked, clothes blew away.

Three children stood beside a low stonewall, spreading clothes out to dry. On each garment they placed a rock. Even then the clothes fluttered like flags and pennants.

Usha, dark-haired, rose-cheeked, struggled with her grandfather's long, loose shirt. She was about eleven or twelve. Her younger brother, Suresh, was doing his best to hold down a bed sheet while Binya, a slightly older girl, Usha's friend and neighbour, was handing them the clothes, one at a time.

Once they were sure everything was on the wall, firmly held down by rocks, they climbed upon the flat stones and sat there for a while, in the wind and the sun, staring across the fields at the ruins on Haunted Hill.

'I must go to the bazaar today,' said Usha.

'I wish I could come too,' said Binya. 'But I have to help with the cows and the housework. Mother isn't well.'

'I can come!' said Suresh. He was always ready to visit the bazaar, which was three miles away on the other side of Haunted Hill.

'No, you can't,' said Usha. 'You must help Grandfather chop wood.'

Their father was in the army, posted in a distant part of the country, and Suresh and his grandfather were the only men in the house. Suresh was eight, chubby and almond-eyed.

'Won't you be afraid to come back alone?' he asked.

'Why should I be afraid?'

'There are ghosts on the hill.'

'I know, but I will be back before it gets dark. Ghosts don't appear during the day.'

'Are there many ghosts in the ruins?' asked Binya.

'Grandfather says so. He says that many years ago—over a hundred years ago—English people lived on the hill. But it was a bad spot, always getting struck by lightning, and they had to move to the next range and build another place.'

'But if they went away, why should there be any ghosts?'

'Because—Grandfather says—during a terrible storm, one of the houses was hit by lightning and everyone in it was killed. Everyone, including the children.'

'Were there many children?'

'There were two of them. A brother and sister. Grandfather says he has seen them many times, when passing through the ruins late at night. He has seen them playing in the moonlight.'

'Wasn't he frightened?'

'No. Old people don't mind seeing ghosts.'

Usha set out on her walk to the bazaar at two in the afternoon. It was about an hour's walk. She went through the fields, now turning yellow with flowering mustard, then along the saddle of the hill, and up to the ruins.

The path went straight through the ruins. Usha knew it well; she had often taken it while going to the bazaar to do the weekly shopping, or to see her aunt who lived in the town.

Wild flowers grew in the crumbling walls. A wild plum tree grew straight out of the floor of what had once been a large hall. Its soft, white blossoms had begun to fall. Lizards scuttled over the stones, while a whistling thrush, its deep-purple plumage glistening in the soft sunshine, sat in an empty window and sang its heart out.

Usha sang to herself, as she tripped lightly along the path. Soon she had left the ruins behind. The path dipped steeply down to the valley and the little town with its straggling bazaar.

Usha took her time in the bazaar. She bought soap and matches, spices and sugar (none of these things could be had in the village, where there was no shop), a new pipe stem for her grandfather's hookah and an exercise book for Suresh to do his sums in. As an afterthought, she bought him some marbles. Then she went to a mochi's shop to have her mother's slippers repaired. The mochi was busy, so she left the slippers with him and said she'd be back in half an hour.

She had two rupees of her own saved up, and she used the money to buy herself a necklace of amber-coloured beads from the old Tibetan lady who sold charms and trinkets at a tiny shop at the end of the bazaar.

There she met her Aunt Lakshmi, who took her home for tea.

Usha spent an hour in Aunt Lakshmi's little flat above the shops, listening to her aunt talk about the ache in her left shoulder and the stiffness in her joints. She drank two cups of sweet, hot tea, and when she looked out of the window she saw that dark clouds had gathered over the mountains.

Usha ran to the cobbler's and collected her mother's slippers. The shopping bag was full. She slung it over her shoulder and set out for the village.

Strangely, the wind had dropped. The trees were still, not a leaf moved. The crickets were silent in the grass. The crows flew round in circles, then settled down for the night in an oak tree.

'I must get home before dark,' said Usha to herself, as she hurried along the path. But already the sky was darkening. The clouds, black and threatening, loomed over Haunted Hill. This was March, the month for storms.

A deep rumble echoed over the hills, and Usha felt the first heavy drop of rain hit her cheek.

She had no umbrella with her; the weather had seemed so fine just a few hours ago. Now all she could do was tie an old scarf over her head and pull her shawl tight across her shoulders. Holding the shopping bag close to her body, she quickened her pace. She was almost running. But the raindrops were coming down faster now. Big, heavy pellets of rain.

A sudden flash of lightning lit up the hill. The ruins stood out in clear outline. Then all was dark again. Night had fallen.

I won't get home before the storm breaks, thought Usha. I'll have to shelter in the ruins. She could only see a few feet ahead, but she knew the path well and began to run.

Suddenly, the wind sprang up again and brought the rain with a rush against her face. It was cold, stinging rain. She could hardly keep her eyes open.

The wind grew in force. It hummed and whistled. Usha did not have to fight against it. It was behind her now, and helped her along, up the steep path and on to the brow of the hill.

There was another flash of lightning, followed by a peal of thunder. The ruins loomed up before her, grim and forbidding.

She knew there was a corner where a piece of old roof remained. It would give some shelter. It would be better than trying to go on. In the dark, in the howling wind, she had only to stray off the path to go over a rocky cliff edge.

Who–whoo–whooo, howled the wind. She saw the wild plum tree swaying, bent double, its foliage thrashing against the ground. The broken walls did little to stop the wind.

Usha found her way into the ruined building, helped by her memory of the place and the constant flicker of lightning. She began moving along the wall, hoping to reach the sheltered corner. She placed her hands flat against the stones and moved sideways. Her hand touched something soft and furry. She gave a startled cry and took her hand away. Her cry was answered by another cry—half snarl, half screech—and something leapt away in the darkness.

It was only a wild cat. Usha realized this when she heard it. The cat lived in the ruins, and she had often seen it. But for a moment, she had been very frightened. Now, she moved quickly along the wall until she heard the rain drumming on the remnant of the tin roof.

Once under it, crouching in the corner, she found some shelter from the wind and the rain. Above her, the tin sheets groaned and clattered, as if they would sail away at any moment. But they were held down by the solid branch of a straggling old oak tree.

Usha remembered that across this empty room stood an old fireplace, and that there might be some shelter under the blocked-up chimney. Perhaps it would be drier than it was in her corner; but she would not attempt to find it just now. She might lose her way altogether.

Her clothes were soaked and the water streamed down from her long, black hair to form a puddle at her feet. She stamped her feet to keep them warm. She thought she heard a faint cry—was it the cat again, or an owl?—But the sound of the storm blotted out all other sounds.

There had been no time to think of ghosts, but now that she was there, without any plans for venturing out again, she remembered Grandfather's story about the lightning-blasted ruins. She hoped and prayed that lightning would not strike *her* as she sheltered there.

Thunder boomed over the hills, and the lightning came quicker now, only a few seconds between each burst.

Then there was a bigger flash than most, and for a second or two the entire ruin was lit up. A streak of blue sizzled along the floor of the building, in at one end and out at the other. Usha was staring straight ahead. As the opposite wall was lit up, she saw, crouching in the disused fireplace, two small figures—they could only have been children!

The ghostly figures looked up, staring back at Usha. And then everything was dark again.

Usha's heart was in her mouth. She had seen, without a shadow of a doubt, two ghostly creatures at the other side of the room, and she wasn't going to remain in that ruined building a minute longer.

She ran out of her corner, ran towards the big gap in the wall through which she had entered. She was halfway across the open space when something—someone—fell against her. She stumbled, got up, and again bumped into something. She gave a frightened scream.

Someone else screamed. And then there was a shout, a boy's shout, and Usha instantly recognized the voice.

'Suresh!'

'Usha!'

'Binya!'

'It's me!'

'It's us!'

They fell into each other's arms, so surprised and relieved that all they could do was laugh and giggle and repeat each other's names. Then Usha said, 'I thought you were ghosts.'

'We thought *you* were a ghost!' said Suresh.

'Come back under the roof,' said Usha.

They huddled together in the corner, chattering excitedly.

'When it grew dark, we came looking for you,' said Binya. 'And then the storm broke.'

'Shall we run back together?' asked Usha. 'I don't want to stay here any longer.'

'We'll have to wait,' said Binya. 'The path has fallen away at one place. It won't be safe in the dark, in all this rain.'

'Then we may have to wait till morning,' said Suresh. 'And I'm feeling hungry!'

The wind and rain continued, and so did the thunder and lightning, but they were not afraid now. They gave each other warmth and confidence. Even the ruins did not seem so forbidding.

After an hour the rain stopped, and although the wind continued to blow, it was now taking the clouds away, so that the thunder grew more distant. Then the wind, too, moved on, and all was silent.

Towards dawn, the whistling thrush began to sing. Its sweet, broken notes flooded the rain-washed ruins with music. 'Let's go,' said Usha. 'Come on,' said Suresh. 'I'm hungry.'

As it grew lighter, they saw that the plum tree stood upright again, although it had lost all its blossoms.

They stood outside the ruins, on the brow of the hill, watching the sky grow pink. A light breeze had sprung up.

When they were some distance from the ruins, Usha looked back and said, 'Can you see something there, behind the wall? It's like a hand waving.'

'I can't see anything,' said Suresh.

'It's just the top of the plum tree,' said Binya.

They were on the path leading across the saddle of the hill.

'Goodbye, goodbye . . .'

Voices on the wind.

'Who said goodbye?' asked Usha.

'Not I,' said Suresh.

'Not I,' said Binya.

'I heard someone calling.'

'It's only the wind.'

Usha looked back at the ruins. The sun had come up and was touching the top of the walls. The leaves of the plum tree shone. The thrush sat there, singing.

'Come on,' said Suresh. *'I'm hungry.'*

'Goodbye, goodbye, goodbye, goodbye . . .' Usha heard them calling. Or was it just the wind?

GHOSTS OF A PEEPUL TREE
SOME MUSINGS

The West has its revenants, its spirits of the dead, lost souls searching for lost loves; but in India, and Asia in general, we have a far greater variety of spooky beings, and there is no corner of our country where you won't come across tales of hauntings and the supernatural. So grow a tulsi plant at your door or window, to keep those negative forces at bay!

The villages of India have always harboured a large variety of ghosts, some of them good, some evil. There are the *prets* and *bhoots*, both the spirits of dead men; and the *churels*, ghosts of women who change their shape after death. Then there is the *pisach*, a sort of hobgoblin; and the *munjia*, a mischievous, and sometimes sinister, evil spirit. One thing they have in common: nearly all of them choose to live in the peepul tree.

There is not much difference between the bhoot and the pret—the latter is simply a better class of ghost, less inclined to indulge in malicious activities. It is usually the spirit of one who has loved the earth so much that he cannot bear to take final leave of it. The pret lives either in its former home or in a peepul tree, and is sometimes honoured by the title of Purwaj Dev, an ancestor god. Prets often take the form of snakes, living in people's gardens, where they are fed with milk and honoured by the household.

* * *

There is a story of a villager who was in the habit of beating his son unceasingly. One day, the villager visited a garden where a Purwaj Dev dwelt in the form of a snake. The serpent threatened to bite and kill the villager unless he promised to treat his son better. The villager went away a chastened man.

The lady of the house was very fond of the snake and gave it milk every day; and in return for this favour, the snake would often guard her baby and rock its cradle.

* * *

A ghost which, in the past, was often responsible for the desertion of a house, or even of a village, was the churel.

A churel is the ghost of a woman who has changed her shape after death. She is full of animosity towards men, probably because, in life, she was unfairly treated by them. She is covered with hair, has the ears of an ape, and her toes are two or three feet in length. Sometimes her feet face backwards. During the day, the churel has no power, but at night, she lies along the branches of a peepul tree, directly over a footpath. Should any man pass beneath the tree, the churel's prehensile toes stretch out, grip the man by the neck and throttle him.

* * *

The pisach can be a malignant, sometimes amorous, ghost. It has no body or shape, but dwells in a peepul tree or a graveyard. In the Vetal Panchvishi, there is the story of a young wife who,

while her husband is in another town, falls in love with a young man. On her husband's return, the wife would have nothing to do with him; as soon as he was asleep, she ran to join her lover near the house of her maidservant. But the lover, who had arrived first, was bitten by a cobra, and died before the woman arrived. A pisach (who had seen everything from a nearby peepul tree) now entered the dead man's body and began to play the lover to the errant wife. After some time, out of sheer wickedness, the pisach bit off the woman's nose, left the corpse and went back to the peepul tree.

The unfortunate lady, now without a nose, ran home screaming that her husband had bitten it off. The husband was arrested, and his execution ordered; but a stranger suggested that a search be made at the maidservant's cottage. There they found the lover's body on the bed, and between his teeth was the wife's nose. Finally, the husband was acquitted, and the wife placed on a donkey and driven out of the city.

* * *

The Marathas used to be familiar with an evil spirit known as munjia.

A munjia is said to be the disembodied spirit of a Brahmin youth who has died before his marriage. Like other spirits, it lives in a peepul tree, often rushing out at tongas, bullock carts and bicycles, and upsetting them. (No instance has as yet been recorded of its trying conclusions with a bus.) When passing a peepul tree at night, should anyone be so careless as to yawn without snapping his fingers in front of his mouth, a munjia will dash down his throat and completely ruin him. It is quite possible that people suffering from indigestion have made the mistake of yawning under a peepul tree.

* * *

It is not surprising that in villages, after dark, everyone is supposed to carry a lamp, even the blind. And if you ask the blind man what use a lamp is to him, he will reply, 'Fool, the lamp is not for my benefit, but yours, lest you stumble against me in the dark.'

Note: This piece first appeared in the *Statesman* in 1961. There is no dearth of prets, churels and pisaches around us. You will encounter many as you turn the pages.

THE HAUNTED BICYCLE

I was living at the time in a village about five miles out of Shahganj, a district in east Uttar Pradesh, and my only means of transport was a bicycle. I could, of course, have gone into Shahganj on any obliging farmer's bullock cart, but, in spite of bad roads and my own clumsiness as a cyclist, I found the bicycle a trifle faster. I went into Shahganj almost every day, collected my mail, bought a newspaper, drank innumerable cups of tea and gossiped with the tradesmen. I cycled back to the village at about six in the evening, along a quiet, unfrequented forest road. During the winter months it was dark by six, and I would have to use a lamp on the bicycle.

One evening, when I had covered about half the distance to the village, I was brought to a halt by a small boy who was standing in the middle of the road. The forest, at that late hour, was no place for a child: wolves and hyenas were common in the district. I got down from my bicycle and approached the boy, but he didn't seem to take much notice of me.

'What are you doing here on your own?' I asked.

'I'm waiting,' he said, without looking at me.

'Waiting for whom? Your parents?'

'No, I am waiting for my sister.'

'Well, I haven't passed her on the road,' I said. 'She may be further ahead. You had better come along with me, we'll soon find her.'

The boy nodded and climbed silently on to the crossbar in front of me. I have never been able to recall his features. Already it was dark and besides, he kept his face turned away from me.

The wind was against us, and as I cycled on, I shivered with the cold, but the boy did not seem to feel it. We had not gone far when the light from my lamp fell on the figure of another child who was standing by the side of the road. This time it was a girl. She was a little older than the boy, and her hair was long and windswept, hiding most of her face.

'Here's your sister,' I said. 'Let's take her along with us.'

The girl did not respond to my smile, and she did no more than nod seriously to the boy. But she climbed up on to my back carrier, and allowed me to pedal off again. Their replies to my friendly questions were monosyllabic, and I gathered that they were wary of strangers. Well, when I got to the village, I would hand them over to the headman, and he could locate their parents.

The road was level, but I felt as though I was cycling uphill. And then I noticed that the boy's head was much closer to my face, that the girl's breathing was loud and heavy, almost as though *she* were doing the riding. Despite the cold wind, I began to feel hot and suffocated.

'I think we'd better take a rest,' I suggested.

'No!' cried the boy and girl together. 'No rest!'

I was so surprised that I rode on without any argument; and then, just as I was thinking of ignoring their demand and stopping, I noticed that the boy's hands, which were resting on the handlebar, had grown long and black and hairy.

My hands shook and the bicycle wobbled about on the road.

'Be careful!' shouted the children in unison.

'Look where you're going!'

Their tone now was menacing and far from childlike. I took a quick glance over my shoulder and had my worst fears confirmed. The girl's face was huge and bloated. Her legs, black and hairy, were trailing along the ground.

'Stop!' ordered the terrible children. 'Stop near the stream!'

But before I could do anything, my front wheel hit a stone, and the bicycle toppled over. As I lay sprawled in the dust, I felt something hard, like a hoof, hit me on the back of the head, and then there was total darkness.

When I recovered consciousness, I noticed that the moon had risen and was sparkling on the waters of the stream. The children were not to be seen anywhere. I got up from the ground and began to brush the dust from my clothes. And then, hearing the sound of splashing and churning, I looked up again.

Two small black buffaloes gazed at me from the muddy, moonlit water.

WOULD ASTLEY RETURN?

The house was called Undercliff because that's where it stood—under a cliff. The man who went away—the owner of the house—was Robert Astley. And the man who stayed behind—the old family retainer—was Prem Bahadur.

Astley had been gone many years. He was still a bachelor in his late thirties when he'd suddenly decided that he wanted adventure, romance and faraway places. He'd given the keys of the house to Prem Bahadur—who'd served the family for thirty years—and had set off on his travels.

Someone saw him in Sri Lanka. He'd been heard of in Burma, around the ruby mines at Mogok. Then he turned up in Java, seeking a passage through the Sunda Straits. After that the trail petered out. Years passed. The house in the hill station remained empty.

But Prem Bahadur was still there, living in an outhouse.

Every day he opened up Undercliff, dusted the furniture in all the rooms, made sure that the bed sheets and pillowcases were clean and set out Astley's dressing gown and slippers.

In the old days, whenever Astley came home after a journey or a long tramp in the hills, he liked to bathe and change into his gown and slippers, no matter what the hour. Prem Bahadur still kept them ready. He was convinced that Robert would return one day.

Astley himself had said so.

'Keep everything ready for me, Prem, old chap. I may be back after a year, or two years, or even longer, but I'll be back, I promise you. On the first of every month, I want you to go to my lawyer, Mr Kapoor. He'll give you your salary and any money that's needed for the rates and repairs. I want you to keep the house tip-top!'

'Will you bring back a wife, sahib?'

'Lord, no! Whatever put that idea in your head?'

'I thought, perhaps—because you wanted the house kept ready . . .'

'Ready for me, Prem. I don't want to come home and find the old place falling down.'

And so Prem had taken care of the house—although there was no news from Astley. What had happened to him? The mystery provided a talking point whenever the local people met on the Mall. And in the bazaar, the shopkeepers missed Astley because he had been a man who spent freely.

His relatives still believed him to be alive. Only a few months back a brother had turned up—a brother who had a farm in Canada and could not stay in India for long. He had deposited a further sum with the lawyer and told Prem to carry on as before. The salary provided Prem with his few needs. Moreover, he was convinced that Robert would return.

Another man might have neglected the house and grounds, but not Prem Bahadur. He had a genuine regard for the absent owner. Prem was much older—now almost sixty and none too strong, suffering from pleurisy and other chest troubles—but he remembered Robert as both a boy and a young man. They had been together on numerous hunting and fishing trips in the mountains. They had slept out under the stars, bathed in icy mountain streams and eaten from the same cooking pot. Once, when crossing a small river, they had been swept downstream by a flash flood, a wall of water that came thundering down the gorges without any warning during the rainy season. Together they had struggled back to safety. Back in the hill station, Astley had told everyone that Prem had saved his life, while Prem was equally insistent that he owed his life to Robert.

* * *

This year the monsoon had begun early and ended late. It dragged on through most of September, and Prem Bahadur's cough grew worse and his breathing more difficult.

He lay on his charpai on the veranda, staring out at the garden, which was beginning to get out of hand, a tangle of dahlias, snake-lilies and convolvuluses. The sun finally came out. The wind shifted from the south-west to the north-west and swept the clouds away.

Prem Bahadur had shifted his charpai into the garden and was lying in the sun, puffing at his small hookah, when he saw Robert Astley at the gate.

He tried to get up but his legs would not oblige him. The hookah slipped from his hand.

Astley came walking down the garden path and stopped in front of the old retainer, smiling down at him. He did not look a day older than when Prem Bahadur had last seen him.

'So you have come at last,' said Prem.

'I told you I'd return.'

'It has been many years. But you have not changed.'

'Nor have you, old chap.'

'I have grown old and sick and feeble.'

'You'll be fine now. That's why I've come.'

'I'll open the house,' said Prem, and this time he found himself getting up quite easily.

'It isn't necessary,' said Astley.

'But all is ready for you!'

'I know. I have heard of how well you have looked after everything. Come then, let's take a last look around. We cannot stay, you know.'

Prem was a little mystified but he opened the front door and took Robert through the drawing room and up the stairs to the bedroom. Robert saw the dressing gown and the slippers, and he placed his hand gently on the old man's shoulder.

When they returned downstairs and emerged into the sunlight, Prem was surprised to see himself—or rather his skinny body—stretched out on the charpai. The hookah was on the ground, where it had fallen.

Prem looked at Astley in bewilderment.

'But who is that—lying there?'

'It was you. Only the husk now, the empty shell. This is the real you, standing here beside me.'

'You came for me?'

'I couldn't come until you were ready. As for me, I left *my* shell a long time ago. But you were determined to hang on, keeping this house together. Are you ready now?'

'And the house?'

'Others will live in it. But come, it's time to go fishing . . .'

Astley took Prem by the arm, and they walked through the dappled sunlight under the deodars and finally left that place forever.

THE PRIZE

They were up late, drinking in the old Ritz bar, and by 1 a.m. everyone was pretty well sloshed. Ganesh got into his electric-blue Zen and zigzagged home. Victor drove off in his antique Morris Minor, which promptly broke down, forcing him to transfer to a taxi.

Nandu, the proprietor, limped off to his cottage, a shooting pain in his foot presaging another attack of gout. Begum Tara, who had starred in over a hundred early talkies, climbed into a cycle rickshaw that had no driver, which hardly mattered, as she promptly fell asleep. The bartender vanished into the night. Only Rahul, the romantic young novelist, remained in the foyer, wondering where everyone had gone and why he had been left behind.

The rooms were full. There wasn't a spare bed in the hotel, for it was the height of the season and the hill station's hotels were overflowing. The room boys and kitchen staff had gone to their quarters. Only the night chowkidar's whistle could occasionally be heard as the retired havildar prowled around the estate.

The young writer felt he had been unfairly abandoned, and rather resented the slight. He'd been the life and soul of the party—or so he'd thought—telling everyone about the huge advance he'd just got for his latest book and how it was a certainty for the Booker Prize. He hadn't noticed their yawns; or if he had, he'd put it down to the lack of oxygen in the bar. It had been named the Horizontal Bar by one of the patrons, because of a tendency on the part of some of the clientele to fall asleep on the carpet—that very same carpet on which the Duke of Savoy had passed out exactly a hundred years ago.

Rahul had no intention of passing out on the floor. But his libations had made lying down somewhere seem quite imperative. A billiard table would have been fine, but the billiard room was locked. He staggered down the corridor; not a sofa or easy chair came into view. Finally, he found a door that opened, leading to the huge empty dining room, now lit only by a single electric bulb.

The old piano did not look too inviting, but the long dining table had been cleared of everything except a curry-stained tablecloth left there to do duty again at breakfast. Rahul managed to hoist himself upon the table and stretch himself out. It made a hard bed, and already stray breadcrumbs were irritating his tender skin, but he was too tired to care. The light bulb directly above him also failed to bother him too much. Although there was no air in the room, the bulb swayed slightly, as though an invisible hand had tapped it gently.

For an hour he slept, a deep dreamless sleep, and then he became vaguely aware of music, voices, footsteps and laughter. Someone was playing the piano. Chairs were pulled back. Glasses tinkled. Knives and forks clattered against dinner plates.

Rahul opened his eyes to find a banquet in progress. On his table—the table he was lying on—now flanked by huge tureens of food! And the diners were seemingly unaware of his presence. The men wore old-fashioned dress-suits with bow ties and high collars; the women wore long flounced dresses with tight bodices that showed their ample bosoms to good advantage. Out of long habit, Rahul's hand automatically reached out for the nearest breast, and for once he did not receive a stinging slap—for the simple reason that his hands, if they were there at all, hadn't moved.

Someone said, 'Roast pig—I've been looking forward to this!' and stuck a knife and fork into Rahul's thigh.

He cried out, or tried to, but no one heard; he could not hear his own voice. He found he could raise his head and look down the length of his body, and he saw he had pig's trotters instead of his own feet.

Someone turned him over and sliced a bit off his rump.

'A most tender leg of pork,' remarked a woman on his left.

A fork jabbed him in the buttocks. Then a giant of a man, top-hatted, with a carving knife in his hand, leant over him. He wore a broad white apron, and on it was written in large letters: CHAIRMAN OF THE JURY. The carving knife glistened in the lamplight.

Rahul screamed and leapt off the table. He fell against the piano, recovered his balance, dashed past the revellers, and out of the vast dining room.

He ran down the silent hotel corridor, banging on all the doors. But none opened to him. Finally, at Room No. 12A—hotels do not like using the number 13—the door gave way. Out of breath, shaking all over, our hero stumbled into the room and bolted the door behind him.

It was a single room with a single bed. The bedclothes appeared to be in some disarray but Rahul hardly noticed. All he wanted was to end the nightmare he had been having and get some sleep. Kicking off his shoes, he climbed into the bed fully dressed.

He had been lying there for at least five minutes, before he realized that he wasn't alone in the bed. There was someone lying beside him, covered by a sheet. Rahul switched on the bedside lamp. Nothing moved, the body lay still. On the sheet, in large letters, were the words: BETTER LUCK NEXT TIME.

He pulled the sheet back and stared down at his own dead self.

THE GHOST WHO GOT IN

It was Grandfather who finally decided that we would have to move to another house.

And it was all because of a pret, a mischievous north Indian ghost, who had been making life difficult for everyone.

Prets usually live in peepul trees, and that's where our little ghost first had his abode—in the branches of a massive old peepul tree which had grown through the compound wall and spread into our garden. Part of the tree was on our side of the wall, part on the other side, shading the main road. It gave the ghost a commanding view of the entire area.

For many years, the pret had lived there quite happily, without bothering anyone in our house. It did not bother me either, and I spent a lot of time in the peepul tree. Sometimes I went there to escape the adults at home, sometimes to watch the road and people who passed by. The peepul tree was cool on a hot day, and the heart-shaped leaves were always revolving in the breeze. This constant movement of the leaves also helped to disguise the movements of the pret, so that I never really knew exactly where he was sitting. But he paid no attention to me. The traffic on the road kept him fully occupied.

Sometimes, when a tonga passed by, he would jump down and frighten the pony, and, as a result, the little pony cart would go rushing off in the wrong direction.

Sometimes he would get into the engine of a car or a bus, which would break down soon afterwards.

And he liked to knock the *sola topees* (pith helmets) off the heads of sahibs or officials, who would wonder how a strong breeze had sprung up so suddenly, only to die down just as quickly. Although this special kind of ghost could make himself felt, and sometimes heard, he was invisible to the human eye.

I was not invisible to the human eye, and often got blamed for some of the pret's pranks. If bicycle riders were struck by mango seeds or apricot stones, they would look up, see a small boy in the branches of the tree and threaten me with dire consequences.

Drivers who went off after parking their cars in the shade would sometimes come back to find their tyres flat. My protests of innocence did not carry much weight. But when I mentioned the pret in the tree, they would look uneasy—either because they thought I must be mad, or because they were afraid of ghosts, especially prets. They would find other things to do and hurry away.

At night no one walked beneath the peepul tree.

It was said that if you yawned beneath the tree, the pret would jump down your throat and ruin your digestion. Our gardener, Chandu, who was always taking sick leave, blamed the pret for his tummy troubles. Once, when yawning, Chandu had forgotten to snap his fingers in front of his mouth, and the ghost had got in without any trouble.

Now Chandu spent most of his time lying on a string bed in the courtyard of his small house. When Grandmother went to visit him, he would start groaning and holding his sides—the pain was so bad. But when she went away, he did not fuss so much. He claimed that the pain did not affect his appetite, and he ate a normal diet, in fact, a little more than normal—the extra amount was meant to keep the ghost happy!

'Well, it isn't our fault,' said Grandfather, who had given permission to the Public Works Department to cut the tree, which had been on our land. They wanted to widen the road, and the tree and a bit of our wall were in the way. So both had to go.

Several people protested, including the Maharaja of Jetpur, who lived across the road and who sometimes asked Grandfather over for a game of tennis.

'That peepul tree has been there for hundreds of years,' he said. 'Who are we to cut it down?'

'We,' said the chief engineer, 'are the PWD'

And not even a ghost can prevail against the wishes of the Public Works Department.

They brought men with saws and axes, and first, they lopped off all the branches, until the poor tree was quite naked. (It must have been at this moment that the pret moved out.) Then they sawed away at the trunk until, finally, the great old peepul came crashing down on the road, bringing down the telephone wires and an electric pole in the process, and knocking a large gap in the maharaja's garden wall.

It took them three days to clear the road, and during that time the chief engineer swallowed a lot of dust and tree pollen. For months afterwards he complained of a choking feeling, although no doctor could ever find anything in his throat.

'It's the pret's doing,' said the maharaja knowingly.

'They should never have cut that tree.'

Deprived of his tree, the pret decided that he would live in our house.

I first became aware of his presence when I was sitting on the veranda steps, reading a novel. A tiny chuckling sound came from behind me. I looked around, but no one was to be seen. When I returned to my book, the chuckling started again. I paid it no attention. Then a shower of rose petals fell softly on to the pages of my open book. The pret wanted me to know he was there!

'All right,' I said. 'So you've come to stay with us. Now let me read.'

He went away then; but as a good pret has to be bad in order to justify his existence, it was not long before he was up to all sorts of mischief.

He began by hiding Grandmother's spectacles.

'I'm sure I put them down on the dining table,' she grumbled.

A little later, they were found balanced on the snout of a wild boar, whose stuffed and mounted head adorned the veranda wall, a memento of Grandfather's youthful hunting exploits. Naturally, I was, at first, blamed for this prank. But a day or two later, when the spectacles disappeared again, only to be found dangling from the bars of the parrot's cage, it was agreed that I was not to blame; for the parrot had once bitten off a piece of my finger, and I did not go near it any more.

The parrot was hanging upside down, trying to peer through one of the lenses. I don't know if they improved his vision, but what he saw certainly made him angry, because the pupils of his eyes went very small and he dug his beak into the spectacle frames, leaving them with a permanent dent. I caught them just before they fell to the floor.

Our parrot must have been psychic, because even without the help of the spectacles, it seemed that he could see the pret. He would keep turning this way and that, lunging out at unseen fingers and protecting his tail from the tweaks of invisible hands. He had always refused to learn to talk, but now he became quite voluble and began to chatter in some unknown tongue, often screaming with rage and rolling his eyes in a frenzy.

'We'll have to give that parrot away,' said Grandmother. 'He gets more bad-tempered by the day.'

Grandfather was the next to be troubled.

He went into the garden one morning to find all his prize sweet peas broken off and lying on the grass. Chandu thought the sparrows had destroyed the flowers, but we didn't think the birds could have finished off every single bloom just before sunrise.

'It must be the pret,' said Grandfather, and I agreed.

The pret did not trouble me much, because he remembered me from his peepul-tree days and knew I resented the tree being cut as much as he did. But he liked to catch my attention, and he did this by chuckling and squeaking near me when I was alone, or whispering in my ear when I was with someone else. Gradually I began to make out the occasional word—he had started learning English!

Uncle Ken, who came to stay with us for long periods when he had little else to do (which was most of the time), was soon to suffer.

He was a heavy sleeper, and once he'd gone to bed, he hated being woken up. So when he came to breakfast looking bleary-eyed and miserable, we asked him if he was feeling all right. 'I couldn't sleep a wink last night,' he complained.

'Whenever I was about to fall asleep, the bedclothes would be pulled off the bed. I had to get up at least a dozen times to pick them off the floor.' He stared suspiciously at me. 'Where were you sleeping last night, young man?'

'In Grandfather's room,' I said. 'I've lent you my room.'

'It's that ghost from the peepul tree,' said Grandmother with a sigh.

'Ghost!' exclaimed Uncle Ken. 'I didn't know the house was haunted.'

'It is now,' said Grandmother. 'First my spectacles, then the sweet peas, and now Ken's bedclothes! What will it be up to next, I wonder?'

We did not have to wonder for long.

There followed a series of minor disasters. Vases fell off tables, pictures fell from walls. Parrots' feathers turned up in the teapot, while the parrot himself let out indignant squawks and swear words in the middle of the night. Windows which had been closed would be found open, and open windows closed.

Finally, Uncle Ken found a crow's nest in his bed, and, on tossing it out of the window, was attacked by two crows.

Then Aunt Ruby came to stay, and things quietened down for a time.

Did Aunt Ruby's powerful personality have an effect on the pret, or was he just sizing her up?

'I think the pret has taken a fancy to your aunt,' said Grandfather mischievously. 'He's behaving himself for a change.'

This may have been true, because the parrot, who had picked up some of the English words being tried out by the pret, now called out, 'Kiss, kiss,' whenever Aunt Ruby was in the room.

'What a charming bird,' said Aunt Ruby.

'You can keep him if you like,' said Grandmother.

One day, Aunt Ruby came into the house, covered in rose petals.

'I don't know where they came from,' she exclaimed. 'I was sitting in the garden, drying my hair, when handfuls of petals came showering down on me!'

'It likes you,' said Grandmother.

'What likes me?'

'The ghost.'

'What ghost?'

'The pret. It came to live in the house when the peepul tree was cut down.'

'What nonsense!' said Aunt Ruby.

'Kiss, kiss!' screamed the parrot.

'There aren't any ghosts, prets or other kinds,' said Aunt Ruby firmly.

'Kiss, kiss!' screeched the parrot again. Or was it the parrot? The sound seemed to be coming from the ceiling.

'I wish that parrot would shut up.'

'It isn't the parrot,' I said. 'It's the pret.'

Aunt Ruby gave me a cuff over the ear and stormed out of the room.

But she had offended the pret. From being her admirer, he turned into her enemy. Somehow her toothpaste got switched with a tube of Grandfather's shaving cream. When she appeared in the dining room, foaming at the mouth, we ran for our lives, Uncle Ken shouting that she'd got rabies.

Two days later, Aunt Ruby complained that she had been struck on the nose by a grapefruit, which had leapt mysteriously from the pantry shelf and hurled itself at her.

'If Ruby and Ken stay here much longer, they'll both have nervous breakdowns,' said Grandfather thoughtfully.

'I thought they broke down long ago,' I said.

'None of your cheek,' snapped Aunt Ruby.

'He's in league with that pret to try and get us out of here,' said Uncle Ken.

'Don't listen to him—you can stay as long as you like,' said Grandmother.

The pret, however, did not feel so hospitable, and the persecution of Aunt Ruby continued.

'When I looked in the mirror this morning,' she complained bitterly, 'I saw a little monster, with huge ears, bulging eyes, flaring nostrils and a toothless grin!'

'You don't look that bad, Aunt Ruby,' I said, trying to be nice.

'It was either you or that imp you call a pret,' said Aunt Ruby. 'And if it's a ghost, then it's time we all moved to another house.'

Uncle Ken had another idea.

'Let's drive the ghost out,' he said. 'I know a sadhu who rids houses of evil spirits.'

'But the pret's not evil,' I said. 'Just mischievous.'

Uncle Ken went off to the bazaar and came back a few hours later with a scruffy-looking sadhu—a sadhu being a man who is supposed to have given up all worldly goods, including most of his clothes. The sadhu prowled about the house and lighted incense in all the rooms, despite squawks of protest from the parrot. All the while he chanted various magic spells. He then collected a fee of thirty rupees and promised that we would not be bothered again by the pret.

As he was leaving, he was suddenly blessed with a shower—no, it was really a downpour—of dead flowers, decaying leaves, orange peels and banana skins. All spells forgotten, he ran to the gate and made for the safety of the bazaar.

Aunt Ruby declared that it had become impossible to sleep at night because of the devilish chuckling that came from beneath her pillow. She packed her bags and left.

Uncle Ken stayed on. He was still having trouble with his bedclothes, and he was beginning to talk to himself, which was a bad sign.

One day, I found him on the drawing-room sofa, laughing like a madman. Even the parrot was so alarmed that it was silent, head lowered, and curious. Uncle Ken was red in the face—literally red all over!

'What happened to your face, Uncle?' I asked.

He stopped laughing and gave me a long, hard look. I realized that there had been no joy in his laughter.

'Who painted the washbasin red without telling me?' he asked in a quavering voice.

'We'll have to move, I suppose,' said Grandfather later. 'Even if it's only for a couple of months. I'm worried about Ken. I've told him that I painted the washbasin myself but forgot to tell him. He doesn't believe me. He thinks it's the pret or the boy, or both of them! Ken needs a change. So do we. There's my brother's house at the other end of the town. He won't be using it for a few months. We'll move in next week.'

And so, a few days and several disasters later, we began moving house.

Two bullock carts laden with furniture and heavy luggage were sent ahead. Uncle Ken went with them. The roof of our old car was piled high with bags and kitchen utensils. Grandfather took the wheel, I sat beside him, and Granny sat in state at the back.

We started off and had gone some way down the main road, when Grandfather started having trouble with the steering wheel. It appeared to have come loose, and the car began veering about on the road, scattering cyclists, pedestrians, stray dogs and hens. A stray cow refused to move, but we missed it somehow—and then suddenly we were off the road and making for a low wall.

Grandfather pressed his foot down on the brake, but we only went faster. 'Watch out!' he shouted.

It was the Maharaja of Jetpur's garden wall, made of single bricks, and the car knocked it down quite easily and went on through it, coming to a stop on the maharaja's lawn.

'Now look what you've done,' said Grandmother.

'Well, we missed the flower beds,' said Grandfather.

'Someone's been tinkering with the car. Our pret, no doubt.'

The maharaja and two attendants came running towards us.

The maharaja was a perfect gentleman, and when he saw that the driver was Grandfather, he beamed with pleasure.

'Delighted to see you, old chap!' he exclaimed. 'Jolly decent of you to drop in. How about a game of tennis?'

'Sorry to have come in through the wall,' apologized Grandfather.

'Don't mention it, old chap. The gate was closed, so what else could you do?'

Grandfather was as much of a gentleman as the maharaja, so he thought it only fair to join him in a game of tennis. Grandmother and I watched and drank lemonades. After the game, the maharaja waved us goodbye and we drove back through the hole in the wall and out on to the road. There was nothing much wrong with the car.

We hadn't gone far when we heard a peculiar sound, as if someone was chuckling and talking to himself. It came from the roof of the car.

'Is the parrot out there on the luggage rack?' asked Grandfather.

'No,' said Grandmother. 'He went ahead with Ken.'

Grandfather stopped the car, got out and examined the roof.

'Nothing up there,' he said, getting in again and starting the engine. 'I thought I heard the parrot.'

When we had gone a little further, the chuckling started again. A squeaky little voice began talking in English, in the tone of the parrot.

'It's the pret,' whispered Grandmother. 'What is he saying?'

The pret's squawk grew louder. 'Come on, come on!' he cried gleefully. 'A new house! The same old friends! What fun we're going to have!'

Grandfather stopped the car. He backed into a driveway, turned round, and began driving back to the old house.

'What are you doing?' asked Grandmother.

'Going home,' said Grandfather.

'And what about the pret?'

'What about him? He's decided to live with us, so we'll have to make the best of it. You can't solve a problem by running away from it.'

'All right,' said Granny. 'But what will we do about Ken?'

'It's up to him, isn't it? He'll be all right if he finds something to do.'

Grandfather stopped the car in front of the veranda steps.

'I'm hungry,' I said.

'It will have to be a picnic lunch,' said Grandmother. 'Almost everything was sent off on the bullock carts.'

As we got out of the car and climbed the veranda steps, we were greeted by showers of rose petals and sweet-scented jasmine. 'How lovely!' exclaimed Grandmother, smiling. 'I think he likes us, after all.'

SUSANNA'S SEVEN HUSBANDS

Locally, the tomb was known as 'the grave of the seven times married one.'

You'd be forgiven for thinking it was Bluebeard's grave; he was reputed to have killed several wives in turn because they showed undue curiosity about a locked room. But this was the tomb of Susanna Anna-Maria Yeates, and the inscription (most of it in Latin) stated that she was mourned by all who had benefited from her generosity, her beneficiaries having included various schools, orphanages and the church across the road. There was no sign of any other graves in the vicinity and presumably, her husbands had been interred in the old Rajpur graveyard, below the Delhi Ridge.

I was still in my teens when I first saw the ruins of what had once been a spacious and handsome mansion. Desolate and silent, its well-laid paths were overgrown with weeds, and its flower beds had disappeared under a growth of thorny jungle. The two-storeyed house had looked across the Grand Trunk Road. Now abandoned, feared and shunned, it stood encircled in mystery, reputedly the home of evil spirits.

Outside the gate, along the Grand Trunk Road, thousands of vehicles sped by—cars, trucks, buses, tractors, bullock carts—but few noticed the old mansion or its mausoleum, set back as they were from the main road, hidden by mango, neem and peepul trees. One old and massive peepul tree grew out of the ruins of the house, strangling it as much as its owner was said to have strangled one of her dispensable paramours.

As a much-married person, with a quaint habit of disposing of her husbands whenever she tired of them, Susanna's malignant spirit was said to haunt the deserted garden. I had examined the tomb, I had gazed upon the ruins, I had scrambled through shrubbery and overgrown rose bushes, but I had not encountered the spirit of this mysterious woman. Perhaps, at the time, I was too pure and innocent to be targeted by malignant spirits. For malignant she must have been, if the stories about her were true.

The vaults of the ruined mansion were rumoured to contain a buried treasure—the amassed wealth of the lady Susanna. But no one dared go down there, for the vaults were said to be occupied by a family of cobras, traditional guardians of buried treasure. Had she really been a woman of great wealth, and could treasure still be buried there? I put these questions to Naushad, the furniture-maker, who had lived in the vicinity all his life, and whose father had made the furniture and fittings for this and other great houses in Old Delhi.

'Lady Susanna, as she was known, was much sought after for her wealth,' recalled Naushad. 'She was no miser, either. She spent freely, reigning in state in her palatial home, with many horses and carriages at her disposal. Every evening she rode through the Roshanara Gardens, the cynosure of all eyes, for she was beautiful as well as wealthy. Yes, all men sought her favours, and she could choose from the best of them. Many were fortune hunters. She did not discourage them. Some found favour for a time, but she soon tired of them. None of her husbands enjoyed her wealth for very long!

'Today no one enters those ruins, where once there was mirth and laughter. She was the Zamindari lady, the owner of much land, and she administered her estate with a strong hand. She was kind if the rent was paid when it was due, but terrible if someone failed to pay.

'Well, over fifty years have gone by since she was laid to rest, but still men speak of her with awe. Her spirit is restless, and it is said that she often visits the scenes of her former splendour. She has been seen walking through this gate, or riding in the gardens, or driving in her phaeton down the Rajpur road.'

'And what happened to all those husbands?' I asked.

'Most of them died mysterious deaths. Even the doctors were baffled. Tomkins Sahib drank too much. The lady soon tired of him. A drunken husband is a burdensome creature, she was heard to say. He would eventually have drunk himself to death, but she was an impatient woman and was anxious to replace him. You see those datura bushes growing wild in the grounds? They have always done well here.'

'Belladonna?' I suggested.

'That's right, huzoor. Introduced in the whisky-soda, it put him to sleep forever.'

'She was quite humane in her way.'

'Oh, very humane, sir. She hated to see anyone suffer. One sahib, I don't know his name, drowned in the tank behind the house, where the water lilies grew. But she made sure he was half-dead before he fell in. She had large, powerful hands, they said.'

'Why did she bother to marry them? Couldn't she just have had men friends?'

'Not in those days, huzoor. Respectable society would not have tolerated it. Neither in India nor in the West would it have been permitted.'

'She was born out of her time,' I remarked.

'True, sir. And remember, most of them were fortune hunters. So we need not waste too much pity on them.'

'She did not waste any.'

'She was without pity. Especially when she found out what they were really after. Snakes had a better chance of survival.'

'How did the other husbands take their leave of this world?'

'Well, the colonel sahib shot himself while cleaning his rifle. Purely an accident, huzoor. Although, some say she had loaded his gun without his knowledge. Such was her reputation by now that she was suspected even when innocent. But she bought her way out of trouble. It was easy enough, if you were wealthy.'

'And the fourth husband?'

'Oh, he died a natural death. There was a cholera epidemic that year, and he was carried off by the *haija*. Although, again, there were some who said that a good dose of arsenic produced the same symptoms! Anyway, it was cholera on the death certificate. And the doctor who signed it was the next to marry her.'

'Being a doctor, he was probably quite careful about what he ate and drank.'

'He lasted about a year.'

'What happened?'

'He was bitten by a cobra.'

'Well, that was just bad luck, wasn't it? You could hardly blame it on Susanna.'

'No, huzoor, but the cobra was in his bedroom. It was coiled around the bedpost. And when he undressed for the night, it struck! He was dead when Susanna came into the room an hour later. She had a way with snakes. She did not harm them and they never attacked her.'

'And there were no antidotes in those days. Exit the doctor. Who was the sixth husband?'

'A handsome man. An indigo planter. He had gone bankrupt when the indigo trade came to an end. He was

hoping to recover his fortune with the good lady's help. But our Susanna Mem, she did not believe in sharing her fortune with anyone.'

'How did she remove the indigo planter?'

'It was said that she lavished strong drinks upon him, and when he lay helpless, she assisted him on the road we all have to take one day, by pouring molten lead in his ears.'

'A painless death, I'm told.'

'But a terrible price to pay, huzoor, simply because one is no longer needed . . .'

We walked along the dusty highway, enjoying the evening breeze, and sometime later we entered the Roshanara Gardens, in those days Delhi's most popular and fashionable meeting place.

'You have told me how six of her husbands died, Naushad. I thought there were seven?'

'Ah, the seventh was a gallant young magistrate who perished right here, huzoor. They were driving through the park after dark, when the lady's carriage was attacked by brigands. In defending her, the young man received a fatal sword wound.'

'Not the lady's fault, Naushad.'

'No, huzoor. But he was a magistrate, remember, and the assailants, one of whose relatives had been convicted by him, were out for revenge. Oddly enough, though, two of the men were given employment by the lady Susanna at a later date. You may draw your own conclusions.'

'And were there others?'

'Not husbands. But an adventurer, a soldier of fortune came along. He found her treasure, they say. And he lies buried with it, in the cellars of the ruined house. His bones lie scattered there, among gold and silver and precious jewels.

The cobras guard them still! But how he perished was a mystery, and remains so till this day.'

'And Susanna? What happened to her?'

'She lived to a ripe old age. If she paid for her crimes, it wasn't in this life! She had no children, but she started an orphanage and gave generously to the poor and to various schools and institutions, including a home for widows. She died peacefully in her sleep.'

'A merry widow,' I remarked. 'The black widow spider!'

Don't go looking for Susanna's tomb. It vanished some years ago, along with the ruins of her mansion. A smart new housing estate came up on the site, but not after several workmen and a contractor succumbed to snakebite! Occasionally, residents complain of a malignant ghost in their midst, who is given to flagging down cars, especially those driven by single men. There have also been one or two mysterious disappearances.

And after dusk, an old-fashioned horse and carriage can sometimes be seen driven through the Roshanara Gardens. If you chance upon it, ignore it, my friend. Don't stop to answer any questions from the beautiful, fair lady who smiles at you from behind lace curtains. She's still looking for her final victim.

EYES OF THE CAT

Her eyes seemed flecked with gold when the sun was on them. And as the sun set over the mountains, drawing a deep, red wound across the sky, there was more than gold in Kiran's eyes. There was anger; for she had been cut to the quick by some remarks her teacher had made—the culmination of weeks of insults and taunts.

Kiran was poorer than most of the girls in her class and could not afford the tuitions that had become almost obligatory if one was to pass and be promoted. 'You'll have to spend another year in the ninth,' said Madam. 'And if you don't like that, you can find another school—a school where it won't matter if your blouse is torn and your tunic is old and your shoes are falling apart.' Madam had shown her large teeth in what was supposed to be a good-natured smile, and all the girls had tittered dutifully. Sycophancy had become part of the curriculum in Madam's private academy for girls.

On the way home in the gathering gloom, Kiran's two companions commiserated with her.

'She's a mean old thing,' said Aarti. 'She doesn't care for anyone but herself.'

'Her laugh reminds me of a donkey braying,' said Sunita, who was more forthright.

But Kiran wasn't really listening. Her eyes were fixed on some point in the far distance, where the pines stood in silhouette against a night sky that was growing brighter every moment. The moon was rising, a full moon, a moon that meant something very special to Kiran, that made her blood tingle and her skin prickle and her hair glow and send out sparks. Her steps seemed to grow lighter, her limbs more sinewy, as she moved gracefully, softly over the mountain path.

Abruptly she left her companions at a fork in the road.

'I'm taking the shortcut through the forest,' she said.

Her friends were used to her sudden whims. They knew she was not afraid of being alone in the dark. But Kiran's moods made them feel a little nervous, and now, holding hands, they hurried home along the open road.

The shortcut took Kiran through the dark oak forest. The crooked, tormented branches of the oaks threw twisted shadows across the path. A jackal howled at the moon; a nightjar called from the bushes. Kiran walked fast, not out of fear but from urgency, and her breath came in short, sharp gasps. Bright moonlight bathed the hillside when she reached her home on the outskirts of the village.

Refusing her dinner, she went straight to her small room and flung the window open. Moonbeams crept over the windowsill and over her arms, which were already covered with golden hair. Her strong nails had shredded the rotten wood of the windowsill.

* * *

Tail swishing and ears pricked, the tawny leopard came swiftly out of the window, crossed the open field behind the house and melted into the shadows.

A little later, it padded silently through the forest.

Although the moon shone brightly on the tin-roofed town, the leopard knew where the shadows were deepest and merged beautifully with them. An occasional intake of breath,

which resulted in a short, rasping cough, was the only sound it made.

Madam was returning from dinner at a ladies' club, called the Kitten Club—a sort of foil to the husbands' club affiliations. There were still a few people in the street, and while no one could help noticing Madam, who had the contours of a steamroller, none saw or heard the predator who had slipped down a side alley and reached the steps of the teacher's house. It sat there silently, waiting with all the patience of an obedient schoolgirl.

When Madam saw the leopard on her steps, she dropped her handbag and opened her mouth to scream; but her voice would not materialize. Nor would her tongue ever be used again, either to savour chicken biryani or to pour scorn upon her pupils, for the leopard had sprung at her throat, broken her neck and dragged her into the bushes.

In the morning, when Aarti and Sunita set out for school, they stopped, as usual, at Kiran's cottage and called out to her.

Kiran was sitting in the sun, combing her long, black hair.

'Aren't you coming to school today, Kiran?' asked the girls.

'No, I won't bother to go today,' said Kiran. She felt lazy, but pleased with herself, like a contented cat.

'Madam won't be pleased,' said Aarti. 'Shall we tell her you're sick?'

'It won't be necessary,' said Kiran, and gave them one of her mysterious smiles. 'I'm sure it's going to be a holiday.'

Her gentle mouth and slender hands were still smeared with blood.

THE TROUBLE WITH JINNS

My friend Jimmy has only one arm. He lost the other when he was a young man of twenty-five. The story of how he lost his good right arm is a little difficult to believe, but I swear that it is absolutely true.

To begin with, Jimmy was (and presumably still is) a jinn. Now, a jinn isn't really a human like us. A jinn is a spirit creature from another world who has assumed, for a lifetime, the physical aspect of a human being. Jimmy was a true jinn and he had the jinn's gift of being able to elongate his arm at will. Most jinns can stretch their arms to a distance of twenty or thirty feet. Jimmy could attain forty feet. His arm would move through space or up walls or along the ground like a beautiful gliding serpent. I have seen him stretched out beneath a mango tree, helping himself to ripe mangoes from the top of the tree. He loved mangoes. He was a natural glutton and it was probably his gluttony that first led him to misuse his peculiar gifts.

We were at school together at a hill station in northern India. Jimmy was particularly good at basketball. He was clever enough not to lengthen his arm too much because he did not want anyone to know that he was a jinn. In the boxing ring, he generally won his fights. His opponents never seemed to get past his amazing reach. He just kept tapping them on the nose until they retired from the ring, bloody and bewildered.

It was during the half-term examinations that I stumbled on Jimmy's secret. We had been set a particularly difficult algebra paper, but I had managed to cover couple of sheets with correct answers and was about to forge ahead on another sheet, when I noticed someone's hand on my desk. At first I thought it was the invigilator's. But when I looked up, there was no one beside me. Could it be the boy sitting directly behind? No, he was engrossed in his question paper and had his hands to himself. Meanwhile, the hand on my desk had grasped my answer sheets and was cautiously moving off. Following its descent, I found that it was attached to an arm of amazing length and pliability. This moved stealthily down the desk and slithered across the floor, shrinking all the while, until it was restored to its normal length. Its owner was, of course, one who had never been any good at algebra.

I had to write out my answers a second time, but after the exam, I went straight up to Jimmy, told him I didn't like his game and threatened to expose him. He begged me not to let anyone know, assured me that he couldn't really help himself, and offered to be of service to me whenever I wished. It was tempting to have Jimmy as my friend, for with his long reach, he would obviously be useful. I agreed to overlook the matter of the pilfered papers and we became the best of pals.

It did not take me long to discover that Jimmy's gift was more of a nuisance than a constructive aid. That was because Jimmy had a second-rate mind and did not know how to make proper use of his powers. He seldom rose above the trivial. He used his long arm in the tuck shop, in the classroom, in the dormitory. And when we were allowed out to the cinema, he used it in the dark of the hall.

Now, the trouble with all jinns is that they have a weakness for women with long, black hair. The longer and blacker the hair, the better for jinns. And should a jinn manage to take possession of the woman he desires, she goes into a decline and her beauty decays. Everything about her is destroyed, except for the beautiful long, black hair.

Jimmy was still too young to be able to take possession in this way, but he couldn't resist touching and stroking long, black hair. The cinema was the best place for the indulgence of his whims. His arm would start stretching, his fingers would feel their way along the rows of seats, and his lengthening limb would slowly work its way along the aisle, until it reached the back of the seat in which sat the object of his admiration. His hand would stroke the long, black hair with great tenderness, and if the girl felt anything and looked around, Jimmy's hand would disappear behind the seat and lie there, poised like the hood of a snake, ready to strike again.

At college two or three years later, Jimmy's first real victim succumbed to his attentions. She was a lecturer in Economics, not very good-looking, but her hair, black and lustrous, reached almost to her knees. She usually kept it in plaits, but Jimmy saw her one morning, just after she had taken a head bath, and her hair lay spread out on the cot on which she was reclining. Jimmy could no longer control himself. His spirit, the very essence of his personality, entered the woman's body, and the next day she was distraught, feverish and excited. She would not eat, went into a coma, and in a few days, dwindled to a mere skeleton. When she died, she was nothing but skin and bone, but her hair had lost none of its loveliness.

I took pains to avoid Jimmy after this tragic event. I could not prove that he was the cause of the lady's sad demise, but in my own heart I was quite certain of it. For, since meeting Jimmy, I had read a good deal about jinns and knew their ways.

We did not see each other for a few years. And then, holidaying in the hills last year, I found we were staying at the same hotel. I could not very well ignore him, and after we had drunk a few beers together, I began to feel that I had perhaps misjudged Jimmy and that he was not the irresponsible jinn I had taken him for. Perhaps the college lecturer had died of some mysterious malady that attacks only college lecturers, and Jimmy had nothing at all to do with it.

We had decided to take our lunch and a few bottles of beer to a grassy knoll just below the main motor-road. It was late afternoon and I had been sleeping off the effects of the beer, when I woke to find Jimmy looking rather agitated.

'What's wrong?' I asked.

'Up there, under the pine trees,' he said.

'Just above the road. Don't you see them?'

'I see two girls,' I said. 'So what?'

'The one on the left. Haven't you noticed her hair?'

'Yes, it is very long and beautiful and—now look, Jimmy, you'd better get a grip on yourself.' But already his hand was out of sight, his arm snaking up the hillside and across the road.

Presently I saw the hand emerge from some bushes near the girls and then cautiously make its way to the girl with the black tresses. So absorbed was Jimmy in the pursuit of his favourite pastime that he failed to hear the blowing of a horn. Around the bend of the road, came a speeding Mercedes-Benz truck.

Jimmy saw the truck but there wasn't time for him to shrink his arm back to normal. It lay right across the entire width of the road, and when the truck had passed over it, it writhed and twisted like a mortally wounded python.

By the time the truck driver and I could fetch a doctor, the arm (or what was left of it) had shrunk to its ordinary size. We took Jimmy to hospital, where the doctors found it necessary to amputate. The truck driver, who kept insisting that the arm he had run over was at least thirty feet long, was arrested on a charge of drunken driving.

Some weeks later I asked Jimmy, 'Why are you so depressed? You still have one arm. Isn't it gifted in the same way?'

'I never tried to find out,' he said, 'and I'm not going to try now.'

He is, of course, still a jinn at heart, and whenever he sees a girl with long, black hair, he must be terribly tempted to try out his one good arm and stroke her beautiful tresses. But he has learnt his lesson. It is better to be a human without any gifts than a jinn or a genius with one too many.

WILSON'S BRIDGE

The old wooden bridge has gone, and today an iron suspension bridge straddles the Bhagirathi as it rushes down the gorge below Gangotri. But villagers will tell you that you can still hear the hoofs of Wilson's horse as he gallops across the bridge he had built a hundred and fifty years ago. At the time, people were sceptical of its safety, and so, to prove its sturdiness, he rode across it again and again. Parts of the old bridge can still be seen on the far bank of the river. And the legend of Wilson and his pretty hill bride, Gulabi, is still well known in this region.

I had joined some friends in the old forest rest house near the river. There were the Rays, recently married, and the Duttas, married many years. The younger Rays quarrelled frequently; the older Duttas looked on with more amusement than concern. I was a part of their group and yet something of an outsider. As a single man, I was a person of no importance. And as a marriage counsellor, I wouldn't have been of any use to them.

I spent most of my time wandering along the riverbanks or exploring the thick deodar and oak forests that covered the slopes. It was these trees that had made a fortune for Wilson and his patron, the Raja of Tehri. They had exploited the great forests to the full, floating huge logs downstream to the timber yards in the plains.

Returning to the rest house late one evening, I was halfway across the bridge, when I saw a figure at the other end, emerging from the mist. Presently I made out a woman, wearing the plain dhoti of the hills; her hair fell loose over her shoulders. She appeared not to see me, and reclined against the railing of the bridge, looking down at the rushing waters far below. And then, to my amazement and horror, she climbed over the railing and threw herself into the river.

I ran forward, calling out, but I reached the railing only to see her fall into the foaming waters below, where she was carried swiftly downstream.

The watchman's cabin stood a little way off. The door was open. The watchman, Ram Singh, fifteen, was reclining on his bed, smoking a hookah.

'Someone just jumped off the bridge,' I said breathlessly. 'She's been swept down the river!'

The watchman was unperturbed. 'Gulabi again,' he said, almost to himself; and then to me, 'Did you see her clearly?'

'Yes, a woman with long, loose hair—but I didn't see her face very clearly.'

'It must have been Gulabi. Only a ghost, my dear sir. Nothing to be alarmed about. Every now and then someone sees her throw herself into the river. Sit down,' he said, gesturing towards a battered old armchair, 'be comfortable and I'll tell you all about it.'

I was far from comfortable, but I listened to Ram Singh tell me the tale of Gulabi's suicide. After making me a glass of hot, sweet tea, he launched into a long, rambling account of how Wilson, a British adventurer seeking his fortune, had been hunting musk deer when he encountered Gulabi on the path from her village. The girl's grey-green eyes and peach-blossom complexion enchanted him, and he went out of his way to get to know her people. Was he in love with her, or did he simply find her beautiful and desirable? We shall never really know. In the course of his travels and adventures, he had known many women, but Gulabi was different—childlike and ingenuous— and he decided he would marry her. The humble family to which she belonged had no objection. Hunting had its limitations, and Wilson found it more profitable to trap the region's great forest wealth. In a few years, he had made a fortune. He built a large timbered house at Harsil, another in Dehradun and a third at Mussoorie. Gulabi had all she could have wanted, including two robust little sons. When he was away on work, she looked after their children and their large apple orchard at Harsil.

And then came the evil day when Wilson met the Englishwoman, Ruth, on the Mussoorie Mall, and decided that she should have a share of his affections and his wealth. A fine house was provided for her too. The time he spent at Harsil with Gulabi and his children dwindled. 'Business affairs'—he was now one of the owners of a bank—kept him in the fashionable hill resort. He was a popular host and took his friends and associates on shikar parties in the Doon.

Gulabi brought up her children in village style. She heard stories of Wilson's dalliance with the Mussoorie woman and, on one of his rare visits, she confronted him and voiced her resentment, demanding that he leave the other woman. He brushed her aside and told her not to listen to idle gossip. When he turned away from her, she picked up the flintlock pistol that lay on the gun table, and fired one shot at him. The bullet missed him and shattered her looking glass. Gulabi ran out of the house, through the orchard and into the forest, then down the steep path to the bridge built by Wilson only two or three years before. When he had recovered his composure, he mounted his horse and came looking for her. It was too late. She had already thrown herself off the bridge into the swirling waters far below. Her body was found a mile or two downstream, caught between some rocks.

This was the tale that Ram Singh told me, with various flourishes and interpolations of his own. I thought it would make a good story to tell my friends that evening, before the fireside in the rest house. They found the story fascinating, but when I told them I had seen Gulabi's ghost, they thought I was doing a little embroidering of my own. Mrs Dutta thought it was a tragic tale. Young Mrs Ray thought Gulabi had been very silly. 'She was a simple girl,' opined Mr Dutta. 'She responded in the only way she knew . . .' 'Money can't buy happiness,' said Mr Ray. 'No,' said Mrs Dutta, 'but it can buy you a great many comforts.' Mrs Ray wanted to talk of other things, so I changed the subject. It can get a little confusing for a bachelor who must spend the evening with two married couples. There are undercurrents which he is aware of but not equipped to deal with.

I would walk across the bridge quite often after that. It was busy with traffic during the day, but after dusk there were only a few vehicles on the road and seldom any pedestrians. A mist rose from the gorge below and obscured the far end of the bridge. I preferred walking there in the evening, half-expecting, half-hoping to see Gulabi's ghost again. It was her face that I really wanted to see. Would she still be as beautiful as she was fabled to be?

It was on the evening before our departure that something happened that would haunt me for a long time afterwards.

There was a feeling of restiveness as our days there drew to a close. The Rays had apparently made up their differences, although they weren't talking very much. Mr Dutta was anxious to get back to his office in Delhi and Mrs Dutta's rheumatism was playing up. I was restless too, wanting to return to my writing desk in Mussoorie.

That evening I decided to take one last stroll across the bridge to enjoy the cool breeze of a summer's night in the mountains. The moon hadn't come up, and it was really quite dark, although there were lamps at either end of the bridge providing sufficient light for those who wished to cross over.

I was standing in the middle of the bridge, in the darkest part, listening to the river thundering down the gorge, when I saw the sari-draped figure emerging from the lamplight and making towards the railings.

Instinctively I called out, 'Gulabi!'

She half-turned towards me, but I could not see her clearly. The wind had blown her hair across her face and all I saw were wildly staring eyes. She raised herself over the railing and threw herself off the bridge. I heard the splash as her body struck the water far below.

Once again, I found myself running towards the part of the railing where she had jumped. And then someone was running towards the same spot, from the direction of the rest house. It was young Mr Ray.

'My wife!' he cried out. 'Did you see my wife?'

He rushed to the railing and stared down at the swirling waters of the river.

'Look! There she is!' He pointed at a helpless figure bobbing about in the water.

We ran down the steep bank to the river, but the current had swept her on. Scrambling over rocks and bushes, we made frantic efforts to catch up with the drowning woman. But the river in that defile is a roaring torrent, and it was over an hour before we were able to retrieve poor Mrs Ray's body, caught in driftwood about a mile downstream.

She was cremated not far from where we found her, and we returned to our various homes in gloom and grief, chastened, but none the wiser for the experience.

If you happen to be in that area and decide to cross the bridge late in the evening, you might see Gulabi's ghost or hear the hoofbeats of Wilson's horse as he canters across the old wooden bridge, looking for her. Or you might see the ghost of Mrs Ray and hear her husband's anguished cry. Or there might be others. Who knows?

GHOSTS OF THE SAVOY

Whose ghost was it that Ram Singh (the Savoy bartender) saw last night? A figure in a long, black cloak, who stood for a few moments in the hotel's dimly lit vestibule, and then moved into the shadows of the old lounge. Ram Singh followed the figure, but there was no one in the lounge and no door or window through which the man (if it was a man) had made his exit.

Ram Singh doesn't tipple; or so he says. Nor is he the imaginative type.

'Have you seen this person—this ghost—before?' I asked him.

'Yes, once. Last winter, when I was passing the ballroom, I heard someone playing the piano. The ballroom door was locked, and I couldn't get in, nor could anyone else. I stood on a ledge and looked through one of the windows, and there was this person—a hooded figure, I could not see the face— sitting on the piano stool. I could hear the music playing, and I tapped on the window. The figure turned towards me, but the hood was empty, there was nothing there to see! I ran to my room and bolted the door. We should sell that piano, sir. There's no one here to play it apart from the ghost.'

Almost any story about this old hotel in Mussoorie has a touch of the improbable about it, even when supported by facts. A previous owner, Mr McClintock, had a false nose— according to Nandu, who never saw it. So I checked with old

Negi, who first came to work in the hotel as a room boy back in 1932 (a couple of years before I was born) and who, almost seventy years and two wives later, looks after the front office. Negi tells me it's quite true.

'I used to take McClintock Sahib his cup of cocoa last thing at night. After leaving his room, I'd dash around to one of the windows and watch him until he went to bed. The last thing he did, before putting the light out, was to remove his false nose and place it on the bedside table. He never slept with it on. I suppose it bothered him whenever he turned over or slept on his face. First thing in the morning, before having his cup of tea, he'd put it on again. A great man, McClintock Sahib.'

'But how did he lose his nose in the first place?' I asked.

'Wife bit it off,' said Nandu.

'No, sir,' said Negi, whose reputation for telling the truth is proverbial. 'It was shot away by a German bullet during First World War. He got the Victoria Cross as compensation.'

'And when he died, was he wearing his nose?' I asked.

'No, sir,' said old Negi, continuing his tale with some relish. 'One morning when I took the sahib his cup of tea, I found him stone dead, without his nose! It was lying on the bedside table. I suppose I should have left it there, but McClintock Sahib was a good man, I could not bear to have the whole world knowing about his false nose. So I stuck it back on his face and then went and informed the manager. A natural death, just a sudden heart attack. But I made sure that he went into his coffin with his nose attached!'

We all agreed that Negi was a good man to have around, especially in a crisis.

McClintock's ghost is supposed to haunt the corridors of the hotel, but I have yet to encounter it. Will the ghost be wearing its nose? Old Negi thinks not (the false nose being man-made), but then, he hasn't seen the ghost at close quarters, only receding into the distance, between the two giant deodars on the edge of the Beer Garden.

A lot of people who enter the Writers' Bar look pretty far gone, and sometimes I have difficulty distinguishing the living from the dead. But the real ghosts are those who manage to slip away without paying for their drinks.

SOMETHING IN THE WATER

I discovered the pool near Rajpur on a hot summer's day some fifteen years ago. It was shaded by close-growing sal trees, and looked cool and inviting. I took off my clothes and dived in.

The water was colder than I had expected. It was an icy, glacial cold. The sun never touched it for long, I supposed. Striking out vigorously, I swam to the other end of the pool and pulled myself up on the rocks, shivering.

But I wanted to swim some more. So I dived in again and did a gentle breaststroke towards the middle of the pool. Something slid between my legs. Something slimy, pulpy. I could see no one, hear nothing. I swam away, but the slippery floating thing followed me. I did not like it. Something curled around my leg. Not an underwater plant. Something that sucked at my foot. A long tongue licked my calf. I struck out wildly, thrust myself away from whatever it was that sought my company. Something lonely, lurking in the shadows. Kicking up spray, I swam like a frightened porpoise fleeing from some terror of the deep.

Safely out of the water, I found a warm, sunny rock and stood there, looking down at the water.

Nothing stirred. The surface of the pool was now calm and undisturbed. Just a few fallen leaves floating around. Not a frog, not a fish, not a water bird in sight. And that in itself seemed strange. For you would have expected some sort of pond life to have been in evidence.

But something lived in the pool, of that I was sure. Something very cold-blooded, colder and wetter than the water. Could it have been a corpse trapped in the weeds? I did not want to know; so I dressed and hurried away.

A few days later I left for Delhi, where I went to work in an ad agency, telling people how to beat the summer heat by drinking fizzy drinks that made you more thirsty. The pool in the forest was forgotten.

It was ten years before I visited Rajpur again. Leaving the small hotel where I was staying, I found myself walking through the same old sal forest, drawn almost irresistibly towards the pool where I had not been able to finish my swim. I was not over-eager to swim there again, but I was curious to know if the pool still existed.

Well, it was there all right, although the surroundings had changed and a number of new houses and other buildings had come up where formerly there had only been wilderness. And there was a fair amount of activity in the vicinity of the pool.

A number of labourers were busy with buckets and rubber pipes, draining water from the pool. They had also dammed off and diverted the little stream that fed it.

Overseeing this operation was a well-dressed man in a white safari suit. I thought, at first, that he was an honorary forest warden, but it turned out that he was the owner of a new school that had been set up nearby.

'Do you live in Rajpur?' he asked.

'I used to . . . Once upon a time . . . Why are you emptying the pool?'

'It's become a hazard,' he said. 'Two of my boys were drowned here recently. Both senior students. Of course, they weren't supposed to be swimming here without permission, the pool is off-limits. But you know what boys are like. Make a rule and they feel duty-bound to break it.'

He told me his name was Kapoor, and led me back to his house, a newly-built bungalow with a wide, cool veranda. His servant brought us glasses of cold sherbet. We sat in cane chairs overlooking the pool and the forest. Across a clearing, a gravelled road led to the school buildings, newly whitewashed and glistening in the sun.

'Were the boys there at the same time?' I asked.

'Yes, they were friends. And they must have been attacked by absolute fiends. Limbs twisted and broken, faces disfigured. But death was due to drowning—that was the verdict of the medical examiner.'

We gazed down at the shallows of the pool, where a couple of men were still at work, the others having gone for their midday meal.

'Perhaps it would be better to leave the place alone,' I said. 'Put a barbed-wire fence around it. Keep your boys away. Thousands of years ago, this valley was an inland sea. A few small pools and streams are all that is left of it.'

'I want to fill it in and build something there. An open-air theatre, maybe. We can always create an artificial pond somewhere else.'

Presently, only one man remained at the pool, knee-deep in muddy, churned-up water. And Mr Kapoor and I both saw what happened next.

Something rose out of the bottom of the pool. It looked like a giant snail, but its head was part-human, its body and limbs part-squid or octopus. An enormous succubi. It stood taller than the man in the pool. A creature soft and slimy, a survivor from our primeval past.

With a great sucking motion, it enveloped the man completely, so that only his arms and legs could be seen thrashing about wildly and futilely. The succubi dragged him down under the water.

Kapoor and I left the veranda and ran to the edge of the pool. Bubbles rose from the green scum near the surface. All was still and silent. And then, like bubblegum issuing from the mouth of a child, the mangled body of the man shot out of the water and came spinning towards us.

Dead and drowned and sucked dry of its fluids.

Naturally, no more work was done at the pool. The story was put out that the labourer had slipped and fallen to his death on the rocks. Kapoor swore me to secrecy. His school would have to close down if there were too many strange drownings and accidents in its vicinity. But he walled the place off from his property and made it practically inaccessible. The dense undergrowth of the sal forest now hides the approach.

The monsoon rains came and the pool filled up again.

I can tell you how to get there if you'd like to see it. But I wouldn't advise you to go for a swim.

THE FAMILY GHOST

'Now tell us a ghost story,' I told Bibiji, my landlady, one evening, as she made herself comfortable on the old couch in the veranda. 'There must have been at least one ghost in your village.'

'Oh, there were many,' said Bibiji, who never tired of telling weird tales. 'Wicked churels and mischievous prets. And there was a munjia who ran away.'

'What is a munjia?' I asked.

'A munjia is the ghost of a Brahmin youth who had committed suicide on the eve of his marriage. Our village munjia had taken up residence in an old peepul tree.'

'I wonder why ghosts always live in peepul trees!' I said.

'I'll tell you about that another time,' said Bibiji. 'But listen to the story about the munjia . . .'

Near the village peepul tree (according to Bibiji), there lived a family of Brahmins who were under the special protection of this munjia. The ghost had attached himself to this particular family (they were related to the girl to whom he had once been betrothed) and showed his fondness for them by throwing stones, bones, night soil and rubbish at them, making hideous noises and terrifying them whenever he found an opportunity. Under his patronage, the family soon dwindled away. One by one they died, the only survivor being an idiot boy, whom the ghost did not bother, because he thought it beneath his dignity to do so.

But, in a village, birth, marriage and death must come to all, and so it was not long before the neighbours began to make plans for the marriage of the idiot.

After a meeting of the village elders, they agreed, first, that the idiot should be married; and second, that he should be married to a shrew of a girl who had reached the age of sixteen without finding a suitor.

The shrew and the idiot were soon married off, and then left to manage for themselves. The poor idiot had no means of earning a living and had to resort to begging. Previously, he had barely been able to support himself, and now his wife was an additional burden. The first thing she did when she entered his house was to give him a box on the ear and send him out to bring something home for their dinner.

The poor fellow went from door to door, but nobody gave him anything, because the same people who had arranged his marriage were annoyed that he had not given them a wedding feast. When, in the evening, he returned home empty-handed, his wife cried out, 'Are you back, you lazy idiot? Where have you been so long, and what have you brought for me?' When she found he hadn't even a paisa, she flew into a rage and, tearing off his turban, threw it into the peepul tree. Then, taking up her broom, she thrashed her husband until he fled from the house, howling with pain.

But the shrew's anger had not yet diminished. Seeing her husband's turban in the peepul tree, she began to beat the tree trunk, accompanying her blows with strong abuses. The ghost who lived in the tree was sensitive to her blows and, alarmed that her language might have the effect of finishing him off altogether, he took to his invisible heels, and left the tree on which he had lived for many years.

Riding on a whirlwind, the ghost soon caught up with the idiot, who was still running down the road leading away from the village.

'Not so fast, brother!' cried the ghost. 'Desert your wife, certainly, but not your old family ghost! The shrew has driven me out of my peepul tree. Truly, a ghost is no match for a woman with a vile tongue! From now on we are brothers and must seek our fortunes together. But first, promise me that you will not return to your wife.'

The idiot made this promise very willingly, and together they continued their journey until they reached a large city.

Before entering the city, the ghost said, 'Now listen, brother, and if you follow my advice, your fortune is made. In this city there are two very beautiful girls, one is the daughter of a raja, and the other the daughter of a rich moneylender. I will go and possess the daughter of the raja and her father will try every sort of remedy without effect. Meanwhile, you must walk daily through the streets in the robes of a sadhu, and when the raja comes and asks you to cure his daughter, make any terms that you think suitable. As soon as I see you, I shall leave the girl. Then I shall go and possess the daughter of the moneylender. But do not go anywhere near her, because I am in love with the girl and do not intend giving her up. If you come near her, I shall break your neck.'

The ghost went off on his whirlwind, and the idiot entered the city on his own, and found a bed in the local rest house for pilgrims.

The next day the city was agog with the news that the raja's daughter was dangerously ill. Physicians—hakims and vaids—came and went, and all pronounced the girl incurable. The raja was distracted with grief, and offered half his fortune to anyone who would cure his beautiful and only child. The idiot, having smeared himself with dust and ashes, began walking the streets, occasionally crying out, '*Bhum, bhum, bho! Bom Bhola Nath!*'

The people were struck by his appearance, and taking him for a wise and holy man, reported him to the raja. The latter immediately entered the city and, prostrating himself before the idiot, begged him to cure his daughter. After a show of modesty and reluctance, the idiot was persuaded to accompany the raja back to the palace, and the girl was brought before him.

Her hair was dishevelled; her teeth were chattering, and her eyes almost starting from their sockets. She howled and cursed and tore at her clothes. When the idiot confronted her, he recited certain meaningless spells; and the ghost, recognizing him, cried out, 'I go, I go! *Bhum, bhum, bho!*'

'Give me a sign that you have gone,' demanded the idiot.

'As soon as I leave the girl,' said the ghost, 'you will see that mango tree uprooted. That is the sign I'll give.'

A few minutes later, the mango tree came crashing down. The girl recovered from her fit and seemed unaware of what had happened to her. The news spread through the city, and the idiot became the object of respect and wonder. The raja kept his word and gave him half his fortune; and so began a period of happiness and prosperity for the idiot.

A few weeks later, the ghost took possession of the moneylender's daughter, with whom he was deeply in love. Seeing his daughter go out of her right senses, the moneylender sent for the highly esteemed idiot and offered him a great sum of money if he would cure his daughter. But remembering the ghost's warning, the idiot refused to go. The moneylender was enraged and sent his henchmen to bring the idiot to him by force; and the idiot, having no means of resisting, was dragged along to the rich man's house.

As soon as the ghost saw his old companion, he cried out in a rage, 'Idiot, why have you broken our agreement and come here? Now I will have to break your neck!'

But the idiot, whose reputation for wisdom had actually served to make him wiser, said, 'Brother ghost, I have not come to trouble you, but to tell you a terrible piece of news. Old friend and protector, we must leave this city soon. You see, SHE has come here—my dreaded wife, the shrew!—to torment us both, and to drag us back to the village. She is on the road to this house and will be here in a few minutes!'

When the ghost heard this, he cried out, 'Oh no, oh no! If she has come, then we must go! *Bhum bho, bhum bho*, we go, we go!'

And breaking down the walls and doors of the house, the ghost gathered himself up into a little whirlwind and went scurrying out of the city, to look for a vacant peepul tree.

The moneylender, delighted that his daughter had been freed of the evil influence, embraced the idiot and showered presents on him.

And in due course, concluded Bibiji, the idiot married the moneylender's beautiful daughter, inherited his father-in-law's wealth and became the richest and most successful moneylender in the city.

THE BAR THAT TIME FORGOT

'Cockroaches!' exclaimed Her Highness, the maharani. 'Cockroaches everywhere! Can't put down my glass without finding a cockroach beneath it!'

'Cockroaches have a special liking for this room,' observed Colonel Wilkie from his corner by the disused fireplace. 'For one thing, our Melaram there—'and he indicated the bartender with a tilt of his double chin—'never washes the glasses properly. And there are sandwich remains all over the place. Last week's sandwiches, I might add. From that party of yours, Vijay.'

Vijay, former Test cricketer, now forty and with a forty-three waist, turned to the colonel. 'You should see the kitchen. A pigsty. The cook is seldom sober.'

'We are seldom sober,' said Suresh Mathur, income-tax lawyer, from his favourite bar stool.

'Speak for yourself,' snapped H.H. 'Simon, fetch me another whisky.'

Simon Lee, secretary-companion to Her Highness, rose dutifully from his chair and took her glass over to the bar counter.

'Indian whisky or Scotch, sir?' asked the bartender in a loud voice, knowing the maharani was too mean to buy Scotch.

'Whisky will do,' said Simon. 'And a beer for me.' Just then he felt like spiking the maharani's whisky with something really lethal and be free of her for the rest of his days. Years of loyalty and companionship had given way to abject slavery, and there was nothing he could do about it. Nearing seventy, unqualified and unworldly, he could hardly set about creating any sort of career for himself.

'And what are you having?' he asked Suresh Mathur, who had just put away his first drink.

'I'm never vague, I ask for Haig!' Suresh replied, chuckling at his clever rhyme. None of the others thought it amusing, but this was usual. 'When they stop giving me credit, I'll try the local stuff.'

'Good on you!' called Colonel Wilkie from his corner. 'But there's nothing to beat Solan No. 1. Don't trust these single malts—they always give me gout!'

'I've never seen you move from that chair,' said Vijay. 'No wonder you suffer from gout.'

'Played cricket once, like you,' said the colonel. 'Made a few runs. But they always made me twelfth man. Got fed up carrying out the drinks, or fielding when the star batsman felt indisposed. Gave up cricket. Indoor games are better. Why don't we have a dartboard in here? In England, every respectable pub has a dartboard.'

I'd been listening to the conversation from a small table behind a potted palm. I was sixteen, just out of school, and I wasn't supposed to be in the bar, even if I wasn't drinking. The large potted palm separated the barroom from the outer lounge; it was neutral territory.

'I have a dartboard!' I piped up, and every head turned towards me. Most of them had been unaware of my presence. They knew, of course, that I was the son of the lady who managed the hotel.

Suresh Mathur, the most literary-inclined of the lot, said, 'Young Copperfield has a dartboard!'

'I'll go and fetch it,' I said, only too ready to justify my presence in the bar.

I dashed down the corridor to my room and collided with my mother, who was doing her nightly round of the hotel.

'What are you doing here? You mustn't hang around the bar,' she said sharply. 'You have a radio in your room, apart from all your books.'

The radio had been given to me the previous year by a guest who was now wanted by the police (on suspicion of being a serial killer), but I did not feel in any way guilty about possessing it; the guest had been very friendly and generous.

'Darts,' I told my mother. 'They want to play darts. That's what a pub is for, isn't it?' And I charged into my room, picked up my old dartboard and set of darts, and returned breathless to the barroom.

My arrival was greeted by cheers, and Vijay helped me find a place for the dartboard, just below a framed picture of winged cherubs sporting about on some unlikely clouds.

'Whoever gets the highest score has a free drink,' announced Vijay.

'Who pays for it?' asked Suresh Mathur.

'We all do—income-tax lawyers included.'

'He never saved anyone a rupee of tax,' declared the maharani. 'But come on, let's have a game.'

'Would you like to start the proceedings, H.H.?'

'No, I'll wait till everyone's finished. You can start with Colonel Wilkie.'

'Age before beauty,' said Vijay. 'Come on, Colonel, we know you have a steady hand.'

Colonel Wilkie's hand was far from steady. His hands were always trembling. But he struggled out of his chair and took up his position at a point indicated by Vijay. Only one

of his darts struck the board, earning him fifteen points. The others were near misses. Two darts bounced off the picture on the wall.

'The old fool's aiming at those naked cherubs,' crowed H.H. 'Go on, Simon, see if you can win a free drink for me.'

Simon did his best, but scored a meagre thirty points.

'Idiot!' cried H.H. 'And you always said you were a good darts player.'

'Out of practice,' Simon mumbled.

Meanwhile, someone had opened up the old radiogram and placed a record on the turntable. The cheeky voice of Maurice Chevalier filled the room:

> *All I want is just one girl,*
> *But I've got to have one girl,*
> *Yes, all I want is one—*
> *All I want is one—*
> *For a start!*

The evening was livening up. Suresh Mathur scored a few points, but it was Vijay who hit the bullseye and claimed a drink on the house.

'Not until I've had my turn,' shouted H.H., and made a grab for the darts.

She flung them at the board at random, missing wildly— so much so that one dart lodged itself in Colonel Wilkie's old felt hat, which was hanging from a peg, while another streaked across the room and narrowly missed the Roman nose of Reggie Bhowmik, ex-actor, who had just entered the room, accompanied by his demure little wife.

Between ex-actor Reggie and former cricketer Vijay, there was no love lost. Both middle-aged and no longer in demand, they were rivals in failure. One spoke of the prejudice and incompetence of the cricket selectors, the other of jealousy in the film industry and his subsequent neglect. Both lived in the past—Vijay recalling the one outstanding innings he had played for the country (before being dropped after a series of failures), Reggie living on memories of his one great romantic role before a sagging waistline and alcohol-coarsened features had led to a rapid decline in his popularity. Somehow they had drifted into the backwater that was Dehra in 1950.

There are some places, no matter how dull or lacking in opportunity, which nevertheless take a grip on the individual— especially the more easy-going types—and hold him in thrall, rendering him unfit for life in a larger, more competitive milieu. Dehra was one such place.

The bar at Green's Hotel was their refuge and their strength. Here they could reminisce, hark back to glory days, even speak optimistically of the future. Colonel Wilkie, Suresh Mathur, Vijay Kapoor, Reggie Bhowmik, H.H.—the maharani—and Simon Lee, were all dropouts, failures in their own way. Had they been busy and successful, they would not have found their way to Green's every evening.

Reggie Bhowmik liked making dramatic entrances, but the maharani was just as fond of being the centre of attention, and wasn't about to give up centre stage to a fading actor.

'A double whisky for Vijay!' she declared. 'He's the only one here who still has a steady hand.'

'You haven't felt my hand,' said Reggie, bearing down on her. 'You missed my nose by a whisker.'

'You'd look better with a scar running down your face,' said H.H. 'Then you might get a role as Frankenstein or the phantom of the opera.'

This touched a raw nerve, as Reggie had been having some difficulty in getting a decent role in recent months. But he snapped back: 'I'll play the phantom on condition you're cast as the fat soprano—then I shall take great pleasure in strangling you.'

'Let's change the subject,' said his wife, Ruby, always ready to pour oil on troubled waters. She moved over to Colonel Wilkie's table and asked, 'How have you been, Colonel?'

'Like an old bus—just about moving, and badly in need of spare parts.'

'Well, have a beer with us—and some French fries if we can get any.'

'Cook's on strike,' said Vijay. 'Only liquid diet today.'

I saw my opportunity and piped up again from behind the potted palm. 'I can boil some eggs for you, if you like!'

There was a stunned silence, broken by Suresh Mathur, who said, sounding a little incredulous, 'Young Master Copperfield can boil an egg!'

Everyone clapped, and Vijay said, 'Copperfield has certainly saved the day for us. First he produces a dartboard, and now he's about to save us from starvation. Go to it, Copperfield!'

Off I went, then, not to boil eggs—there weren't any in the kitchen—but to find Sitaram, the room boy, who was the only person of my age in the hotel. I found him in my room, listening to 'Binaca Geet Mala', the popular musical request programme, on my radio.

'We need some eggs,' I told him. 'Boiled.'

'Egg-man comes tomorrow,' he said. 'Cook finished the rest. Made himself an omelette, got drunk and took off!'

'Well, let's go down to the bazaar and buy some eggs. I've got enough money on me.'

So off we went and, near the clock tower, found a street vendor selling boiled eggs. We bought a dozen and hurried back to the barroom, where Vijay and Reggie were having a heated argument on the relative merits of cricket and football.

Reggie didn't think much of cricket, and Vijay didn't think much of football.

'And what's your favourite game?' asked Ruby of Suresh Mathur.

'Snakes and ladders,' he said, chuckling, and returned to his drink.

'Boiled eggs!' I announced. 'On the house!'

Sitaram produced saucers, and distributed the eggs among the guests—two each, exactly.

'Do I have to peel my own egg?' asked the maharani querulously, staring down at the two eggs rolling about on her plate. 'Peel them for me, Simon!'

Simon dutifully cracked one of the eggs and began peeling it for her. 'Not that way, you fool. You're leaving all the skin on it.' And seizing the half-peeled egg from her companion, she flung it across the room, narrowly missing the bartender.

'Good throw!' exclaimed Vijay. 'You'd be great fielding on the boundary.'

'Better at baseball,' said Reggie.

'Snakes and ladders,' said Suresh again, now quite drunk.

Colonel Wilkie, equally drunk, gave a loud belch.

The maharani got up to leave. 'Well, I'm not going to sit here to be insulted by everyone. Come on, Simon, drive me home!' And she marched out of the room with an attempt at majesty, but tripped over the hotel cat, an ugly, striped creature who had sensed that there was food around and had come looking for it. The cat caterwauled, H.H. screamed and cursed, Reggie cheered and Suresh Mathur pronounced, 'When two cats are fighting, they make a hideous sound.'

Not to be outdone in nastiness, the maharani went up to Suresh, looked him up and down, and said, 'It's easy to tell you're a single man.'

'I'm not homosexual,' said Suresh defensively. (The word 'gay' had yet to be used in any sense other than 'happy' in those days.)

'No.' The maharani smiled wickedly. 'You're single because you are so damn ugly!'

And on that triumphant note she left the room, followed by the obedient Simon.

'Pay no attention to her, Suresh,' said Vijay generously. 'You're better-looking than that old lapdog who follows her around.'

'I understand she's leaving him her fortunes,' said Reggie. 'I could do with some of it myself. Perhaps I could interest her in producing a film.'

'She's tight-fisted,' said Vijay. 'If you look closely at Simon, you'll notice he's wearing the late maharaja's smoking jacket and deer-stalker cap. The old maharaja loved dressing up like Sherlock Holmes.'

Colonel Wilkie came out of his reverie. 'When I was in Jamnagar—' he began.

'We've heard that a hundred times,' said Vijay.

'I haven't,' said Ruby.

'When I was in Jamnagar,' continued Colonel Wilkie, 'I saw Duleepsinhji made a hundred. That was against Lord Tennyson's team.'

'Yesterday you said Ranjitsinhji,' remarked Vijay.

'I'm not that old,' said Colonel Wilkie, struggling to his feet. 'But old enough to want to go to bed. I'll toddle off now.' Locating his walking stick, he found his way to the door, wishing everyone goodnight as he passed them. They heard the tap of his walking stick as he walked away, down the corridor.

'Shouldn't someone go with him?' asked Ruby. 'It's very late and he isn't too steady on his feet.'

'Oh, he'll find his way home,' said Suresh nonchalantly. 'Lives just around the corner, in rented rooms near the Club.'

'Why doesn't he join the Club?'

'Can't afford it. Neither can I.'

'Neither can I,' said Vijay.

'Neither can we,' added Ruby, sadly. 'And anyway, it's more homely here. Even when the maharani is around.'

'She can afford the Club,' said Suresh. 'But they won't let her in. Created a disturbance once too often. Insulted the secretary and emptied a dish of chicken biryani on his head.'

'Not done,' said Vijay. 'Not cricket.'

'I don't believe it,' said Reggie. 'Can't be true.'

'Calling me a liar?' asked Suresh, bristling.

Ruby poured oil on troubled waters again. 'Interesting if true,' she said. 'And if not true, still interesting.'

'Mark Twain.'

My mother came along the corridor just as Vijay had shown off his knowledge of literature and found me behind the palms, listening to all this fascinating talk.

'Time you went to your room, young man,' she said.

'I'm waiting for everyone to go home,' I said. 'Then I'll help Sitaram tidy up. There's no cook, as you know.'

'Let him stay,' called Suresh from his bar stool. 'It's all part of his education. And he's old enough for a glass of beer. How old are you, sonny?'

'Sixteen,' I said.

'Well, enjoy yourself. It's later than you think.'

But I wasn't thinking of beer just then. I knew there were sausages in the fridge, and I had every intention of polishing them off as soon as all the guests had gone. I wanted to be a writer, but I had no intention of starving in a garret. However, all thoughts of food vanished when I looked across the room and saw Colonel Wilkie framed in the opposite doorway.

He was staring at us through the glass. The glass door then opened of its own volition, and Colonel Wilkie stepped into the room. We all looked up, and Reggie said, 'Back again, Colonel? Still feeling thirsty?' But Colonel Wilkie ignored the jibe and walked slowly across the room to the table where he had been sitting. This was close to where I was standing. He bent down and picked up his pipe from the table. He'd forgotten it when he'd left the barroom. Shoving the pipe into his pocket, he turned and retraced his steps, leaving the room by the door from which he had entered.

'Well, I'm blowed,' said Vijay. 'I thought he was sleep-walking.'

'Never goes anywhere without his pipe,' said Suresh. 'A perfect example of single-mindedness.'

'Didn't say a word.'

'The pipe was all that mattered.'

'Like a favourite cricket bat,' said Vijay.

'Maybe I'll come back for mine when I'm dead.'

A silence fell upon the room. The mention of death had a sobering effect upon the small group. And come to think of it, Colonel Wilkie, on his return to the barroom, had something of the zombie about him—the walking dead.

There was a commotion in the passageway, and my mother burst into the room, followed by the nightwatchman.

'Colonel Wilkie's dead,' said my mother. 'He collapsed on his steps about half an hour ago.'

'But he was here five minutes ago,' said Vijay.

'No, sir,' said Gopal the watchman. 'I went home with him when he left here some time back. Madam said to keep an eye on him. When we got to his place, he began climbing his steps with some difficulty. I helped him to the top step, and then he collapsed. I dragged him into his room and then ran for Dr Bhist. He is there now.'

There was silence for a couple of minutes, and then Ruby said, 'We all saw him. Colonel Wilkie.'

'We saw his ghost,' Vijay murmured.

'He came for his pipe,' said Suresh quietly. 'I told you he wouldn't go anywhere without it.'

Colonel Wilkie was buried the next day, and we made sure his pipe was buried with him. We did not want him turning up from time to time, looking for it. It could be a bit unnerving for the customers.

In all the excitement, I'd forgotten about the sausages, but decided they would keep until after the funeral.

All the regular barflies turned up for the funeral. H.H. was quite sloshed when she arrived and had to be extricated from an open grave into which she had slipped, the ground being soft and yielding after recent rain. She blamed Secretary Simon for the mishap and called him an *'ullu ka pattha'*—son of an owl—but he was quite used to such broadsides and took them in his stride. Was it love or loyalty or dependence that kept him in abeyance? Or was it, as some said, the prospect of becoming her heir? If so, he was paying a heavy price well in advance of such a prospect. Not everyone relishes being abused and kicked around in public by a half-crazed maharani.

When Colonel Wilkie's coffin was lowered into the grave, we all said 'Cheers!' He would have liked that. We then returned to Green's for an early opening of the bar. Alcoholics Unanimous held a subdued but not too melancholy meeting.

But bad news was in store for everyone. A day or two later, I heard the owner, our Sardarji, inform my mother that the hotel had been sold and that she'd have to leave at the end of the month. She'd been expecting something like this and had already accepted a matron's job at one of the schools in the valley. As for me, I was to be packed off to England, to my aunt's home in Jersey. The prospect did not thrill me, but I was more or less resigned to it. And there did not appear to be much future for me in Dehra.

Even before the month was out, workers had begun pulling down parts of the building. It was to be rebuilt as a cinema hall, and would show the latest hits from Bombay. It was even rumoured that Dilip Kumar, the biggest star of that era, would inaugurate the new cinema when it was ready to open.

The spirit and character of a building lasts only while the building lasts. Remove the roof beams, pull down the walls, smash the stairways, and you are left with nothing but memories. Even the ghosts have nowhere to go.

An old hotel that once had a personality of its own was now dismantled with startling rapidity. It had gone up slowly, brick by brick; it came down like a house of cards. No treasures cascaded from its walls; no skeletons were discovered. In two or three days the demolishers had wiped out the past, removed Green's Hotel from the face of the earth so effectively that it might never have existed.

Searching through the ruins one day, I found a bottle opener lying in the dust, and kept it as a souvenir.

The bar had been the only common factor in the lives of those disparate individuals who had come there so regularly—drawn to the place rather than to each other.

Now they went their different ways—Suresh Mathur to the Club, the maharani to her card table and private bar, Vijay to a public school as cricket coach, Reggie Bhowmik and Ruby to Darjeeling to make a documentary . . . Sitaram continued to work for my mother, so I had his company whenever he was free.

The cinema came up quite rapidly, but I had left for England before it opened. When I returned five years later, it was showing Madhubala and Guru Dutt in a romantic comedy, *Mr & Mrs 55*.

Then I moved to Delhi.

In recent years, some of the old single cinemas have been closing down, giving way to multiplexes. The other day, passing through Dehra, I saw that 'our' cinema hall was being pulled down.

'What now?' I asked my taxi driver. 'A multiplex?'

'No, sir. A shopping mall!'

And such is progress.

I think I'm the only one around who is old enough to remember the old Green's Hotel, its dusty corridors, shabby barroom and oddball customers. All have gone. All forgotten! Not even footprints in the sands of time. But by putting down this memoir of an evening or two at that forgotten watering place, I think I have cheated Time just a little.

THE BLACK CAT

Before the cat came, of course there had to be a broomstick. In the bazaar of one of our hill stations is an old junk shop—dirty, dingy and dark—in which I often potter about, looking for old books or Victorian bric-a-brac. Sometimes one comes across useful household items, but I do not usually notice these. I was, however, attracted to an old but well-preserved broom standing in a corner of the shop. A long-handled broom was just what I needed. I had no servant to sweep out the rooms of my cottage, and I did not enjoy bending over double when using the common short-handled *jharoo*.

The old broom was priced at ten rupees. I haggled with the shopkeeper and got it for five.

It was a strong broom, full of character, and I used it to good effect almost every morning. And there this story might have ended—or would never have begun—if I had not found the large, black cat sitting on the garden wall.

The black cat had bright yellow eyes, and it gave me a long, penetrating look, as though it were summing up my possibilities as an exploitable human. Though it miaowed once or twice, I paid no attention. I did not care much for cats. But when I went indoors, I found that the cat had followed and begun scratching at the pantry door.

It must be hungry, I thought, and gave it some milk.

The cat lapped up the milk, purring deeply all the while, then sprang up on a cupboard and made itself comfortable.

Well, for several days, there was no getting rid of that cat. It seemed completely at home, and merely tolerated my presence in the house. It was more interested in my broom than in me, and would dance and skittle around the broom whenever I was sweeping the rooms. And when the broom was resting against the wall, the cat would sidle up to it, rubbing itself against the handle and purring loudly.

A cat and a broomstick—the combination was suggestive, full of possibilities . . . The cottage was old—almost a hundred years old—and I wondered about the kind of tenants it might have had during these long years. I had been in the cottage only for a year. And though it stood alone in the midst of a forest of Himalayan oaks, I had never encountered any ghosts or spirits.

* * *

Miss Bellows came to see me in the middle of July. I heard the tapping of a walking stick on the rocky path outside the cottage, a tapping which stopped near the gate.

'Mr Bond!' called an imperious voice. 'Are you at home?'

I had been doing some gardening, and looked up to find an elderly straight-backed English woman peering at me over the gate.

'Good evening,' I said, dropping my hoe.

'I believe you have my cat,' said Miss Bellows.

Though I had not met the lady before, I knew her by name and reputation. She was the oldest resident in the hill station.

'I do have a cat,' I said, 'though it's probably more correct to say that the cat has me. If it's your cat, you're welcome to it. Why don't you come in while I look for her?'

Miss Bellows stepped in. She wore a rather old-fashioned black dress, and her ancient but strong walnut stick had two or three curves in it and a knob instead of a handle.

She made herself comfortable in an armchair while I went in search of the cat. But the cat was on one of her mysterious absences, and though I called for her in my most persuasive manner, she did not respond. I knew she was probably quite near. But cats are like that—perverse, obstinate creatures.

When finally I returned to the sitting room, there was the cat, curled up on Miss Bellows's lap.

'Well, you've got her, I see. Would you like some tea before you go?'

'No, thank you,' said Miss Bellows. 'I don't drink tea.'

'Something stronger, perhaps. A little brandy?' She looked up at me rather sharply.

Disconcerted, I hastened to add, 'Not that I drink much, you know. I keep a little in the house for emergencies. It helps ward off colds and things. It's particularly good for—er—well, for colds,' I finished lamely.

'I see your kettle's boiling,' she said. 'Can I have some hot water?'

'Hot water? Certainly.' I was a little puzzled, but I did not want to antagonize Miss Bellows at our first meeting.

'Thank you. And a glass.'

She took the glass and I went to get the kettle. From the pocket of her voluminous dress, she extracted two small packets, similar to those containing chemists' powders. Opening both packets, she poured first a purple powder and then a crimson powder into the glass. Nothing happened.

'Now the water, please,' she said.

'It's boiling hot!'

'Never mind.'

I poured boiling water into her glass, and there was a terrific fizzing and bubbling as the frothy stuff rose to the rim. It gave off a horrible stench. The potion was so hot that I thought it would crack the glass; but before this could happen, Miss Bellows put it to her lips and drained the contents.

'I think I'll be going now,' she said, putting the glass down and smacking her lips. The cat, tail in the air, voiced its agreement. Said Miss Bellows, 'I'm much obliged to you, young man.'

'Don't mention it,' I said humbly. 'Always at your service.'

She gave me her thin, bony hand, and held mine in an icy grip.

I saw Miss Bellows and the black cat to the gate, and returned pensively to my sitting room. Living alone was beginning to tell on my nerves and imagination. I made a half-hearted attempt to laugh at my fancies, but the laugh stuck in my throat. I couldn't help noticing that the broom was missing from its corner.

I dashed out of the cottage and looked up and down the path. There was no one to be seen. In the gathering darkness I could hear Miss Bellows's laughter, followed by a snatch of song:

> *With the darkness round me growing,*
> *And the moon behind my hat,*
> *You will soon have trouble knowing*
> *Which is witch and witch's cat.*

Something whirred overhead like a Diwali rocket.

I looked up and saw them silhouetted against the rising moon. Miss Bellows and her cat were riding away on my broomstick.

WHISTLING IN THE DARK

The moon was almost at the full. Bright moonlight flooded the road. But I was stalked by the shadows of the trees, by the crooked oak branches reaching out towards me—some threateningly, others as though they needed companionship.

Once, I dreamt that the trees could walk. That on moonlit nights like this they would uproot themselves for a while, visit each other, talk about old times—for they had seen many men and happenings, especially the older ones. And then, before dawn, they would return to the places where they had been condemned to grow. Lonely sentinels of the night. And this was a good night for them to walk. They appeared eager to do so: a restless rustling of leaves, the creaking of branches— these were sounds that came from within them in the silence of the night . . .

Occasionally, other strollers passed me in the dark. It was still quite early, just eight o'clock, and some people were on their way home. Others were walking into town for a taste of the bright lights, shops and restaurants. On the unlit road, I could not recognize them. They did not notice me. I was reminded of an old song from my childhood. Softly, I began humming the tune, and soon the words came back to me:

We three,
We're not a crowd;

We're not even company—
My echo,
My shadow,
And me . . .

I looked down at my shadow, moving silently beside me. We take our shadows for granted, don't we? There they are, the uncomplaining companions of a lifetime, mute and helpless witnesses to our every act of commission or omission. On this bright, moonlit night I could not help noticing you, Shadow, and I was sorry that you had to see so much that I was ashamed of; but glad, too, that you were around when I had my small triumphs. And what of my echo? I thought of calling out to see if my call came back to me; but I refrained from doing so, as I did not wish to disturb the perfect stillness of the mountains or the conversations of the trees.

The road wound up the hill and levelled out at the top, where it became a ribbon of moonlight entwined between tall deodars. A flying squirrel glided across the road, leaving one tree for another. A nightjar called. The rest was silence.

The old cemetery loomed up before me. There were many old graves—some large and monumental—and there were a few recent graves too, for the cemetery was still in use. I could see flowers scattered on one of them—a few late dahlias and scarlet salvia. Further on, near the boundary wall, part of the cemetery's retaining wall had collapsed in the heavy monsoon rains. Some of the tombstones had come down with the wall. One grave lay exposed. A rotting coffin and a few scattered bones were the only relics of someone who had lived and loved like you and me.

Part of the tombstone lay beside the road, but the lettering had worn away. I am not normally a morbid person, but something made me stoop and pick up a smooth, round

shard of bone, probably part of a skull. When my hand closed over it, the bone crumbled into fragments. I let them fall to the grass. Dust to dust.

And from somewhere, not too far away, came the sound of someone whistling.

At first I thought it was another late-evening stroller, whistling to himself, much as I had been humming my old song. But the whistler, approached quite rapidly; the whistling was loud and cheerful. A boy on a bicycle sped past. I had only a glimpse of him, before his cycle went weaving through the shadows on the road.

But he was back again in a few minutes. And this time, he stopped a few feet away from me and gave me a quizzical half-smile. A slim, dusky boy of fourteen or fifteen. He wore a school blazer and a yellow scarf. His eyes were pools of liquid moonlight.

'You don't have a bell on your cycle,' I said.

He said nothing, just smiled at me with his head a little to one side. I put out my hand, and I thought he was going to take it. But then, quite suddenly, he was off again, whistling cheerfully though rather tunelessly. A whistling schoolboy. A bit late for him to be out, but he seemed an independent sort.

The whistling grew fainter, and then faded away altogether. A deep, sound-denying silence fell upon the forest. My shadow and I walked home.

* * *

Next morning I woke to a different kind of whistling—the song of the thrush outside my window.

It was a wonderful day, the sunshine warm and sensuous, and I longed to be out in the open. But there was work to be done, proofs to be corrected, letters to be written. And it was several days before I could walk to the top of the hill, to that lonely, tranquil resting place under the deodars. It seemed to me ironic that those who had the best view of the glistening snow-capped peaks were all buried several feet underground.

Some repair work was going on. The retaining wall of the cemetery was being shored up, but the overseer told me that there was no money to restore the damaged grave. With the help of the chowkidar, I returned the scattered bones to a little hollow under the collapsed masonry, and I left some money with him so that he could have the open grave bricked up.

The name on the gravestone had worn away, but I could make out a date—20 November 1950—some fifty years ago, but not too long ago as gravestones go . . .

I found the burial register in the church vestry and turned back the yellowing pages to 1950, when I was just a schoolboy myself. I found the name there—Michael Dutta, aged fifteen—and the cause of death: road accident.

Well, I could only make guesses. And to turn conjecture into certainty, I would have to find an old resident who might remember the boy or the accident.

There was old Miss Marley at Pine Top. A retired teacher from Woodstock, she had a wonderful memory, and she had lived in the hill station for more than half a century.

White-haired and smooth-cheeked, her bright blue eyes full of curiosity; she gazed benignly at me through her old-fashioned pince-nez.

'Michael was a charming boy—full of exuberance, always ready to oblige. I had only to mention that I needed a newspaper or an aspirin, and he'd be off on his bicycle, swooping down these steep roads with great abandon. But these hill roads, with their sudden corners, weren't meant for racing around on a bicycle.

'They were widening our road for motor traffic, and a truck was coming uphill, loaded with rubble, when Michael came round a bend and smashed headlong into it. He was rushed to the hospital, and the doctors did their best, but he did not recover consciousness. Of course, you must have seen his grave. That's why you're here. His parents? They left shortly afterwards. Went abroad, I think . . . A charming boy, Michael, but just a bit too reckless. You'd have liked him, I think.'

* * *

I did not see the phantom bicycle-rider again for some time, although I felt his presence on more than one occasion. And when on a cold winter's evening, I walked past that lonely cemetery, I thought I heard him whistling far away. But he did not manifest himself. Perhaps it was only the echo of a whistle, in communion with my insubstantial shadow.

It was several months before I saw that smiling face again. And then it came at me, out of the mist, as I was walking home in drenching monsoon rain. I had been to a dinner party at the old community centre, and I was returning home along a very narrow, precipitous path known as the Eyebrow. A storm had been threatening all evening. A heavy mist had settled on the hillside. It was so thick that the light from my torch simply bounced off it. The sky blossomed with sheet lightning, and thunder rolled over the mountains. The rain became heavier. I moved forward slowly, carefully, hugging the hillside. There was a clap of thunder, and then I saw him emerge from the mist and stand in my way—the same slim, dark youth who had materialized near the cemetery. He did not smile. Instead, he put up his hand and waved me back. I hesitated, stood still. The mist lifted a little, and I saw that the path had disappeared. There was a gaping emptiness a few feet in front of me. And then a drop of over a hundred feet to the rocks below.

As I stepped back, clinging to a thorn bush for support, the boy vanished. I stumbled back to the community centre and spent the night on a chair in the library.

* * *

I did not see him again.

But weeks later, when I was down with a severe bout of flu, I heard him from my sickbed, whistling beneath my window. Was he calling to me to join him, I wondered, or was he just trying to reassure me that all was well? I got out of bed and looked out, but I saw no one. From time to time I heard his whistling; but as I got better, it grew fainter, until it ceased altogether.

Fully recovered, I renewed my old walks to the top of the hill. But although I lingered near the cemetery until it grew dark, and paced up and down the deserted road, I did not see or hear the whistler again. I felt lonely, in need of a friend, even if it was only a phantom bicycle-rider. But there were only the trees.

And so every evening, I walk home in the darkness, singing the old refrain:

> *We three,*
> *We're not alone;*
> *We're not even company—*
> *My echo,*
> *My shadow,*
> *And me . . .*

WHEN THE CLOCK STRIKES THIRTEEN

Tick-tock,
Tick-tock,
One day the clock will strike thirteen, and I'll be liberated forever, thought Rani-ma, as the clock struck twelve and she poured herself another generous peg from the vodka bottle. Recently she had changed from gin to vodka, the latter seemed a little more suited to her mid-morning depression. The bottle was half-empty but it would take her through to the late afternoon, when her ancient manservant, Bahadur, would arrive with another bottle and some vegetables for the evening meal. She did not bother with breakfast or lunch, and yet she was fat, fifty, and oh so forlorn.

Living alone on the seventh floor of a new apartment building—Ranipur's only skyscraper—had only emphasized Rani-ma's loneliness and isolation. Friends had drifted away over the years. Her selfish nature and acerbic tongue had destroyed many relationships. There were no children, for marriage had passed her by. Occasionally a nephew or cousin turned up, hoping for a loan, but going away disappointed.

Rani-ma had nothing to live for, and almost every day, after the third vodka, she contemplated suicide. If only that clock would strike thirteen, Time, for her, would stop, and she would take that fatal leap into oblivion. Because it had to be a leap—something dramatic, something final. No sleeping tablets for her, no overdose of alprax, no hyoscine in her vodka. And she was far too clumsy to try slitting her own wrists; she'd only make a mess of it, and Bahadur would find her bleeding on the carpet and run for a doctor.

There was an old shotgun in the bottom drawer of a cupboard and a case full of cartridges, but the gun hadn't been used for years and the cartridges looked damp and mouldy; of no use, except to frighten off an intruder. No, there was only one thing to do: leap off her seventh-floor balcony, stay airborne for a few seconds, and then—oblivion!

Why wait for that clock to strike thirteen?

Time would never stop—not for her, not for all those thousands below, hurrying about in a heat of hope, striving to find some meaning in their lives, some sustenance for their hordes of children; some happy, some miserable but alive . . .

She opened the door to her balcony and stood there, unsteady, supporting herself against the low railing. Down below on the busy street, cars, scooters, cyclists, pedestrians, went about their business, unaware of the woman looking down upon them from her balcony. Once the queen of Ranipur, she had always looked down upon them. Now her rule extended no further than her apartment, and the world went by, unheeding.

Tick-tock, tick-tock, why keep listening to that wretched clock? Time must have a stop.

* * *

Walking along the pavement with a jaunty air, hat at an angle, humming an old tune, came Colonel Jolly, recently retired. He was on his way to the bank to collect his pension, and he enjoyed walking into town, nodding or waving to acquaintances, stopping occasionally to buy a paper or an ice cream, for he was still a boy as far as ice creams went. He was

enjoying his retirement, his sons were settled abroad, his wife was at home, baking a cake for his evening tea. She was in love with life and he hadn't a care in the world.

As he passed below the tall apartment building, something came between him and the sun, blocking out his vision. He had no idea what it was that struck him, bringing about a total eclipse. One moment, he was striding along, at peace with the world; the next, he was flat on the pavement, buried beneath a mountain of flesh that had struck him like a comet.

Both the colonel and Rani-ma were rushed to the nearest hospital. The colonel's neck and spine had been shattered and he died without recovering consciousness. Rani-ma took some time to recover; but thanks to her fall having been cushioned by the poor colonel, recover she did, retiring to a farmhouse on the outskirts of the town.

Colonel Jolly, lover of life, had lost his to a cruel blow of fate. Rani-ma, who hated living, survived into a grumpy old age.

She is still waiting for the clock to strike thirteen.

THE LONELY GHOST

Mr Lobo wasn't thrown out. His gift as a pianist must have been appreciated by H.H., because two or three evenings later, as I walked past Hollow Oak, I heard the tinkle of a piano and recognized the immortal strains of 'When Irish Eyes Are Smiling', the only thing Irish about H.H. and Mr Lobo being the whisky they had obviously been drinking. It was Irish disguised as Scotch and bottled in Bijnor. Not from Ricardo's cellars.

They were duetting in a grand manner a la Nelson Eddy and Jeanette MacDonald, and while Mr Lobo had a pleasing tenor voice, Neena's raucous strains took all the mystery out of 'Ah! Sweet Mystery of Life'. Tender romance was not her forte.

I continued on my way, stopping at Mrs Montalban's for a mid-morning coffee. Here I learnt that Mr Montalban would be back in a few days, with the intention of spending some time with his family and, of course, 'our wonderful friend, the maharani'.

I found Pablo on the front veranda. He was holding Anna's doll—Anna's birthday doll, the one that supposedly resembled the maharani—and he was busy sticking drawing pins into various parts of its anatomy.

'Drawing pins won't work,' I said. 'You need something with greater penetration.'

He wasn't put out by my intrusion.

'I've got a hammer and nails,' he said, his eyes lighting up. 'Or I could take out all the stuffing.'

'Anna wouldn't like that. Disemboweling her favourite doll.'

'It's not her favourite doll. She doesn't come near it. Actually, she's not into dolls. Prefers ghosts.'

'Ghosts?'

'She keeps seeing a little girl who wants to play with her.'

'Yes, she drew a picture of her. I thought it was just a girl she'd imagined. Have you seen her?'

He shook his head; a lock of hair fell across his brow, giving him a tender, innocent look. Not the sort who practises voodoo on dolls.

'Only Anna has seen her.'

'Perhaps she's a real girl, but very shy. And she runs away, like a frightened gazelle.'

'The old mali says the house is haunted.'

The old mali was an eighty-year-old gardener who did odd jobs at various houses on the hillside. According to him, all the old houses were haunted.

'And what else does he say? That someone died here in tragic circumstances. Most people die at home, you know. It would be hard to find an old house which hadn't been witness to a death or two. Why aren't hospitals haunted? People die in them every day.'

'My mother says some people like to return to their old homes from time to time. They won't go back to a hospital.'

'Don't blame them. Hospitals are scary places—even for ghosts.'

As the evening wore on, Pablo took out his guitar and began strumming it without actually settling into a tune.

'Play something simple,' I said.

And for the first time I heard him singing. It was an old lullaby—something out of Africa, I think. I put it down in words that I remember, for he sang it first in Spanish and then in English:

> *How can there be a cherry without a stone?*
> *How can there be a chicken without a bone?*
> *How can there be a baby with no crying?*
> *How can there be a story with no ending?*
> *And then the answer to this gentle riddle:*
> *A cherry, when it's blooming, it has no stone,*
> *A chicken, when it's hatching, it has no bone,*
> *A baby, when it's sleeping, has no crying . . .*
> *A story of 'I love you' has no ending . . .*

'You sing better than you play,' I said. 'You must sing more often.'

He began singing softly in Spanish, and presently we were joined by Anna and Mrs Montalban. She poured me a glass of red wine and placed a currant cake before me. Normally, I wasn't a wine drinker, but it went well in that house and in that company.

The sun went down with a lot of fuss. First a fiery red, and then in waves of pink and orange as it slid beneath the small clouds that wandered about on the horizon. The brief twilight of northern India passed like a shadow over the hills, and dusk gave way to darkness. I had stepped outside to watch the sunset. Now a lamp came on in the sitting room, followed by the veranda light. An atmosphere of peace and harmony descended on the hillside.

Pablo was calling me. 'Amigo, come quickly. Pronto, pronto!' Whenever he was excited, he broke into Spanish.

I stepped back into the room to find him pointing at the far wall.

A faint glow had spread across the whitewashed wall, as though a part of that spectacular sunset had been left behind. And emerging from this suffused light, as though a rent in the clouds, was the face of a girl. Old-fashioned, sad-happy, beautiful.

'It's her!' exclaimed Anna. 'I've seen her at the window sometimes. And now she's *inside*!'

'She means no harm,' said Mrs Montalban, as composed and unruffled as always. 'She wants to be back here, she longs to be with us—a happy family!'

And it *was* a happy family, in Montalban's prolonged absence.

But the face on the wall soon faded, returned to its own eternal twilight. Who was she, and why had she come back? Perhaps Mrs Montalban was right, and she longed to be of this world again.

We would never know—until and unless we joined her.

A JOB WELL DONE

Dhuki, the gardener, was clearing up the weeds that grew in profusion around the old, disused well. He was an old man, skinny and bent and spindly legged, but he had always been like that. His strength lay in his wrists and in his long, tendril-like fingers. He looked as frail as a petunia but he had the tenacity of a vine.

'Are you going to cover the well?' I asked. I was eight, and a great favourite of Dhuki's. He had been the gardener long before my birth, had worked for my father until my father died and now worked for my mother and stepfather.

'I must cover it, I suppose,' said Dhuki. 'That's what the Major Sahib wants. He'll be back any day and if he finds the well still uncovered, he'll get into one of his raging fits and I'll be looking for another job!'

The 'Major Sahib' was my stepfather, Major Summerskill. A tall, hearty, back-slapping man, who liked polo and pig-sticking. He was quite unlike my father. My father had always given me books to read. The major said I would become a dreamer if I read too much, and took the books away. I hated him and did not think much of my mother for marrying him.

'The boy's too soft,' I heard him tell my mother. 'I must see that he gets riding lessons.'

But before the riding lessons could be arranged, the major's regiment was ordered to Peshawar. Trouble was expected from some of the frontier tribes. He was away for about two months. Before leaving, he had left strict instructions for Dhuki to cover up the old well.

'Too damned dangerous having an open well in the middle of the garden,' my stepfather had said. 'Make sure that it's completely covered by the time I get back.'

Dhuki was loath to cover up the old well. It had been there for over fifty years, long before the house had been built. In its walls lived a colony of pigeons. Their soft cooing filled the garden with a lovely sound. And during the hot, dry summer months, when taps ran dry, the well was always a dependable source of water. The *bhisti* still used it, filling his goatskin bag with the cool, clear water and sprinkling the paths around the house to keep the dust down.

Dhuki pleaded with my mother to let him leave the well uncovered.

'What will happen to the pigeons?' he asked.

'Oh, surely they can find another well,' said my mother. 'Do close it up soon, Dhuki. I don't want the sahib to come back and find that you haven't done anything about it.'

My mother seemed just a little bit afraid of the major. How can we be afraid of those we love? It was a question that puzzled me then and puzzles me still.

The major's absence made life pleasant again. I returned to my books, spent long hours in my favourite banyan tree, ate buckets of mangoes and dawdled in the garden, talking to Dhuki.

Neither he nor I were looking forward to the major's return. Dhuki had stayed on after my mother's second marriage only out of loyalty to her and affection for me. He had really been my father's man. But my mother had always appeared deceptively frail and helpless, and most men, Major Summerskill included, felt protective towards her. She liked people who did things for her.

'Your father liked this well,' said Dhuki. 'He would often sit here in the evenings with a book in which he made drawings of birds and flowers and insects.'

I remembered those drawings and I remembered how they had all been thrown away by the major when he had moved into the house. Dhuki knew about it too. I didn't keep much from him.

'It's a sad business, closing this well,' said Dhuki again. 'Only a fool or a drunkard is likely to fall into it.'

But he had made his preparations. Planks of sal wood, bricks and cement were neatly piled up around the well.

'Tomorrow,' said Dhuki. 'Tomorrow I will do it. Not today. Let the birds remain for one more day. In the morning, baba, you can help me drive the birds from the well.'

On the day my stepfather was expected back, my mother hired a tonga and went to the bazaar to do some shopping. Only a few people had cars in those days. Even colonels went about in tongas. Now, a clerk finds it beneath his dignity to sit in one.

As the major was not expected before evening, I decided I would make full use of my last free morning. I took all my favourite books and stored them away in an outhouse, where I could come for them from time to time. Then, my pockets bursting with mangoes, I climbed up the banyan tree. It was the darkest and coolest place on a hot day in June.

From behind the screen of leaves that concealed me, I could see Dhuki moving about near the well. He appeared to be most unwilling to get on with the job of covering it up.

'Baba!' he called several times. But I did not feel like stirring from the banyan tree. Dhuki grasped a long plank of wood and placed it across one end of the well. He started hammering. From my vantage point in the banyan tree, he looked very bent and old.

A jingle of tonga bells and the squeak of unoiled wheels told me that a tonga was coming in at the gate. It was too early for my mother to be back. I peered through the thick, waxy leaves of the tree and nearly fell off my branch in surprise. It was my stepfather, the major! He had arrived earlier than expected.

I did not come down from the tree. I had no intention of confronting my stepfather until my mother returned.

The major had climbed down from the tonga and was watching his luggage being carried on to the veranda. He was red in the face and the ends of his handlebar moustache were stiff with brilliantine.

Dhuki approached with a half-hearted salaam.

'Ah, so there you are, you old scoundrel!' exclaimed the major, trying to sound friendly and jocular. 'More jungle than garden, from what I can see. You're getting too old for this sort of work, Dhuki. Time to retire! And where's the memsahib?'

'Gone to the bazaar,' said Dhuki.

'And the boy?'

Dhuki shrugged. 'I have not seen the boy today, sahib.'

'Damn!' said the major. 'A fine homecoming, this. Well, wake up the cook boy and tell him to get some sodas.'

'Cook boy's gone away,' said Dhuki.

'Well, I'll be double damned,' said the major.

The tonga went away and the major started pacing up and down the garden path. Then he saw Dhuki's unfinished work at the well. He grew purple in the face, strode across to the well and started ranting at the old gardener.

Dhuki began making excuses. He said something about a shortage of bricks, the sickness of a niece, unsatisfactory cement, unfavourable weather, unfavourable gods. When none of this seemed to satisfy the major, Dhuki began mumbling about something bubbling up from the bottom of the well and pointed down into its depths. The major stepped on to the low parapet and looked down. Dhuki kept pointing. The major leant over a little.

Dhuki's hand moved swiftly, like a conjurer making a pass. He did not actually push the major. He appeared merely to tap him once on the bottom. I caught a glimpse of my stepfather's boots as he disappeared into the well. I couldn't help thinking of *Alice in Wonderland*, of Alice disappearing down the rabbit hole. There was a tremendous splash and the pigeons flew up, circling the well thrice before settling on the roof of the bungalow.

By lunchtime—or tiffin, as we called it then—Dhuki had the well covered over with the wooden planks.

'The major will be pleased,' said my mother when she came home. 'It will be quite ready by evening, won't it, Dhuki?'

By evening the well had been completely bricked over. It was the fastest bit of work Dhuki had ever done.

Over the next few weeks, my mother's concern changed to anxiety, her anxiety to melancholy, and her melancholy to resignation. By being gay and high-spirited myself, I hope I did something to cheer her up. She had written to the colonel of the regiment and had been informed that the major had gone home on leave a fortnight previously. Somewhere, in the vastness of India, the major had disappeared.

It was easy enough to disappear and never be found. After seven months had passed without the major turning up, it was presumed that one of two things must have happened. Either he had been murdered on the train and his corpse flung into a river; or, he had run away with a tribal girl and was living in some remote corner of the country.

Life had to carry on for the rest of us. The rains were over and the guava season was approaching.

My mother was receiving visits from a colonel of His Majesty's 32nd Foot. He was an elderly, easy-going, seemingly

absent-minded man, who didn't get in the way at all but left slabs of chocolate lying around the house.

'A good sahib,' observed Dhuki, as I stood beside him behind the bougainvillea, watching the colonel saunter up the veranda steps. 'See how well he wears his sola topee! It covers his head completely.'

'He's bald underneath,' I said.

'No matter. I think he will be all right.'

'And if he isn't,' I said, 'we can always open up the well again.'

Dhuki dropped the nozzle of the hosepipe and water gushed out over our feet. But he recovered quickly and, taking me by the hand, led me across to the old well, now surmounted by a three-tiered cement platform which looked rather like a wedding cake.

'We must not forget our old well,' he said. 'Let us make it beautiful, baba. Some flowerpots, perhaps.'

And together we fetched pots and decorated the covered well with ferns and geraniums. Everyone congratulated Dhuki on the fine job he'd done. My only regret was that the pigeons had gone away.

HANGING AT THE MANGO TOPE

The two captive policemen, Inspector Hukam Singh and Sub-Inspector Guler Singh, were being pushed unceremoniously along the dusty, deserted, sun-drenched road. The people of the village had made themselves scarce. They would reappear only when the dacoits went away.

The leader of the dacoit gang was Mangal Singh Bundela, great grandson of a Pindari adventurer who had been a thorn in the side of the British. Mangal was doing his best to be a thorn in the flesh of his own government. The local police force had been strengthened recently but it was still inadequate for dealing with the dacoits who knew the ravines better than any surveyor. The dacoit Mangal had made a fortune out of ransom. His chief victims were the sons of wealthy industrialists, moneylenders and landowners. But today he had captured two police officials; of no value as far as ransom went, but prestigious prisoners who could be put to other uses . . .

Mangal Singh wanted to show off in front of the police. He would kill at least one of them—his reputation demanded it—but he would let the other go, in order that his legendary power and ruthlessness be given maximum publicity. A legend is always a help!

His red-and-green turban was tied rakishly to one side. His dhoti extended right down to his ankles. His slippers were embroidered with gold-and-silver thread. His weapon was not

an ancient matchlock but a well-greased .303 rifle. Two of his men had similar rifles. Some had revolvers. Only the smaller fry carried swords or country-made pistols. Mangal Singh's gang, though traditional in many ways, was up-to-date in the matter of weapons. Right now they had the policemen's guns too.

'Come along, Inspector Sahib,' said Mangal Singh, in tones of police barbarity, tugging at the rope that encircled the stout inspector's midriff. 'Had you captured me today, you would have been a hero. You would have taken all the credit, even though you could not keep up with your men in the ravines. Too bad you chose to remain sitting in your jeep with the sub-inspector. The jeep will be useful to us. You will not. But I would like you to be a hero all the same, and there is none better than a dead hero!'

Mangal Singh's followers doubled up with laughter. They loved their leader's cruel sense of humour.

'As for you, Guler Singh,' he continued, giving his attention to the sub-inspector, 'you are a man from my own village. You should have joined me long ago. But you were never to be trusted. You thought there would be better pickings in the police, didn't you?'

Guler Singh said nothing, simply hung his head and wondered what his fate would be. He felt certain that Mangal Singh would devise some diabolical and fiendish method of dealing with his captives. Guler Singh's only hope was Constable Ghanshyam, who hadn't been caught by the dacoits because, at the time of the ambush, he had been in the bushes, relieving himself.

'To the mango tope,' said Mangal Singh, prodding the policemen forward.

'Listen to me, Mangal,' said the perspiring inspector, who was ready to try anything to get out of his predicament. 'Let me go, and I give you my word there'll be no trouble for you in this area as long as I am posted here. What could be more convenient than that?'

'Nothing,' said Mangal Singh. 'But your word isn't good. My word is different. I have told my men that I will hang you at the mango tope and I mean to keep my word. But I believe in fair play—I like a little sport! You may yet go free if your friend here, Sub-Inspector Guler Singh, has his wits about him.'

The inspector and his subordinate exchanged doubtful, puzzled looks. They were not to remain puzzled for long. On reaching the mango tope, the dacoits produced a good, strong hempen rope, one end looped into a slip knot. Many a garland of marigolds had the inspector received during his mediocre career. Now, for the first time, he was being garlanded with a hangman's noose. He had seen hangings, he had rather enjoyed them, but he had no stomach for his own. The inspector begged for mercy. Who wouldn't have, in his position?

'Be quiet,' commanded Mangal Singh. 'I do not want to know about your wife and your children and the manner in which they will starve. You shot my son last year.'

'Not I!' cried the inspector. 'It was some other.'

'You led the party. But now, just to show you that I'm a sporting fellow, I am going to have you strung up from this tree and then I am going to give Guler Singh six shots with a rifle, and if he can sever the rope that suspends you before you are dead, well then, you can remain alive and I will let you go! For your sake I hope the sub-inspector's aim is good. He will have to shoot fast. My man Phambiri, who has made this noose, was once the executioner in a city jail. He guarantees that you won't last more than fifteen seconds at the end of his rope.'

Guler Singh was taken to a spot about forty yards away. A rifle was thrust into his hands. Two dacoits clambered into the branches of the mango tree. The inspector, his hands tied behind, could only gaze at them in horror. His mouth opened and shut as though he already had need of more air. And then, suddenly, the rope went taut, up went the inspector, his throat caught in a vice, while the branch of the tree shook and mango blossoms fluttered to the ground. The inspector dangled from the rope, his feet about three feet above the ground.

'You can shoot,' said Mangal Singh, nodding to the sub-inspector.

And Guler Singh, his hands trembling a little, raised the rifle to his shoulder and fired three shots in rapid succession. But the rope was swinging violently and the inspector's body was jerking about like a fish on a hook. The bullets went wide.

Guler Singh found the magazine empty. He reloaded, wiped the stinging sweat from his eyes, raised the rifle again, took more careful aim. His hands were steadier now. He rested the sights on the upper portion of the rope, where there was less motion. Normally he was a good shot but he had never been asked to demonstrate his skill in circumstances such as these.

The inspector still gyrated at the end of his rope. There was life in him yet. His face was purple. The world, in those choking moments, was a medley of upside-down roofs and a red sun spinning slowly towards him.

Guler Singh's rifle cracked again. An inch or two wide this time. But the fifth shot found its mark, sending small tuffs of rope winging into the air.

The shot did not sever the rope; it was only a nick.

Guler Singh had one shot left. He was quite calm. The rifle sight followed the rope's swing, less agitated now that the inspector's convulsions were lessening. Guler Singh felt sure he could sever the rope this time.

And then, as his finger touched the trigger, an odd, disturbing thought slipped into his mind, stayed there, throbbing: Whose life are you trying to save? Hukam Singh has stood in the way of your promotion more than once. He had you charge-sheeted for accepting fifty rupees from an unlicensed rickshaw puller. He makes you do all the dirty work, blames you when things go wrong, takes the credit when there is credit to be taken. But for him, you'd be an inspector!

The rope swayed slightly to the right. The rifle moved just a fraction to the left. The last shot rang out, clipping a sliver of bark from the mango tree.

The inspector was dead when they cut him down.

'Bad luck,' said Mangal Singh Bundela. 'You nearly saved him. But the next time I catch up with you, Guler Singh, it will be your turn to hang from the mango tree. So keep well away! You know that I am a man of my word. I keep it now by giving you your freedom.'

A few minutes later, the party of dacoits had melted away into the late-afternoon shadows of the scrub forest. There was the sound of a jeep starting up. Then silence—a silence so profound that it seemed to be shouting in Guler Singh's ears.

As the village people began to trickle out of their houses, Constable Ghanshyam appeared, as if from nowhere, swearing that he had lost his way in the jungle. Several people had seen the incident from their windows. They were unanimous in praising the sub-inspector for his brave attempt to save his superior's life. He had done his best.

It is true, thought Guler Singh. I did my best.

That moment of hesitation before the last shot, the question that had suddenly reared up in the darkness of his mind, had already gone from his memory. We remember only what we want to remember.

'I did my best,' he told everyone.

And so he had.

THE GOOD OLD DAYS

I took Miss Mackenzie an offering of a tin of Malabar sardines, and so lessened the sharpness of her rebuke.

'Another doctor's visit, is it?' she said, looking reproachfully at me over her spectacles. 'I might have been dead all this time . . .'

Miss Mackenzie, at eighty-five, did not show the least signs of dying. She was the oldest resident of the hill station. She lived in a small cottage halfway up a hill. The cottage, like Longfellow's village of Attri, gave one the impression of having tried to get to the top of the hill and failed halfway up. It was hidden from the road by oaks and maples.

'I've been away,' I explained. 'I had to go to Delhi for a fortnight. I hope you've been all right?'

I wasn't a relative of Miss Mackenzie's, nor a very old friend; but she had the knack of making people feel they were somehow responsible for her.

'I can't complain. The weather's been good, and the padre sent me some eggs.' She set great store on what was given to her in the way of food. Her pension of forty rupees a month only permitted a diet of dal and rice; but the thoughtfulness of people who knew her, and the occasional gift parcel from England, lent variety to her diet and frequently gave her a topic of conversation.

'I'm glad you have some eggs,' I said. 'They're four rupees a dozen now.'

'Yes, I know. And there was a time when they were only six annas a dozen.'

'About thirty years ago, I suppose.'

'No, twenty-five. I remember, May Taylor's eggs were always the best. She lived in Fairville—the old house near the raja's estate.'

'Did she have a poultry farm?'

'Oh, no, just her own hens. Very ordinary hens, too, not White Leghorns or Rhode Island Red—but they gave lovely eggs, she knew how to keep her birds healthy . . . May Taylor was a friend of mine. She didn't supply eggs to just anybody, you know.'

'Oh, naturally not. Miss Taylor's dead now, I suppose?'

'Oh, yes, quite dead. Her sister saw to that.'

'Oh!' I sensed a story. 'How did that happen?'

'Well, it was a bit of a mystery, really. May and Charlotte never did get on with each other and it's a wonder they agreed to live together. Even as children they used to fight. But Charlotte was always the spoilt one—prettier, you see. May, when I knew her, was thirty-five, a good woman if you know what I mean. She saw to the house and saw to the meals and she went to church like other respectable people and everyone liked her. But Charlotte was moody and bad-tempered. She kept to herself—always had done, since the parents died. And she was a little too fond of the bottle.'

'Neither of them were married?'

'No—I suppose that's why they lived together. Though I'd rather live alone myself than put up with someone disagreeable. Still, they were sisters. Charlotte had been a gay young thing once, very popular with the soldiers at the convalescent home. She refused several offers of marriage, and then when she thought it time to accept someone, there were no more offers. She was almost thirty by then. That's when she started drinking—heavily, I mean. Gin and brandy, mostly. It was cheap in those days. Gin, I think, was two rupees a bottle.'

'What fun! I was born a generation too late.'

'And a good thing, too. Or you'd probably have ended up as Charlotte did.'

'Did she get delirium tremens?'

'She did nothing of the sort. Charlotte had a strong constitution.'

'And so have you, Miss Mackenzie, if you don't mind my saying so.'

'I take a drop when I can afford it—' She gave me a meaningful look. 'Or when I'm offered . . .'

'Did you sometimes have a drink with Miss Taylor?'

'I did not! I wouldn't have been seen in her company. All over the place she was when she was drunk. Lost her powers of discrimination. She even took up with a barber! And then she fell down a khud one evening, and broke her ankle!'

'Lucky it wasn't her head.'

'No, it wasn't her own head she broke, more's the pity, but her sister May's—the poor, sweet thing.'

'She broke her sister's head, did she?' I was intrigued. 'Why, did May find out about the barber?'

'Nobody knows what it was, but it may well have been something like that. Anyway, they had a terrible quarrel one night. Charlotte was drunk, and May, as usual, was admonishing her.'

'Fatal,' I said. 'Never admonish a drunk.'

Miss Mackenzie ignored me and carried on.

'She said something about the vengeance of God falling on Charlotte's head. But it was May's head that was rent asunder. Charlotte flew into a sudden rage—she was given to these outbursts even when sober—and brought something

heavy down on May's skull. Charlotte never said what it was. It couldn't have been a bottle, unless she swept up the broken pieces afterwards. It may have been a heavy—what writers sometimes call a blunt instrument.

'When Charlotte saw what she had done, she went out of her mind. They found her two days later, wandering about near some ruins, babbling a lot of nonsense about how she might have been married long ago if May hadn't clung to her.'

'Was she charged with murder?'

'No, it was all hushed up. Charlotte was sent to the asylum at Ranchi. We never heard of her again. May was buried here. If you visit the old cemetery, you'll find her grave on the second tier, third from the left.'

'I'll look it up some time. It must have been an awful shock for those of you who knew the sisters.'

'Yes, I was quite upset about it. I was very fond of May. And then, of course, the chickens were sold and I had to buy my eggs elsewhere and they were never so good. Still, those were the days, the good old days—when eggs were six annas a dozen, and gin only two rupees a bottle!'

HE SAID IT WITH ARSENIC

Is there such a person as a born murderer—in the sense that there are born writers and musicians, born winners and losers? One can't be sure. The urge to do away with troublesome people is common to most of us but only a few succumb to it.

If ever there was a born murderer, he must surely have been William Jones. The thing came so naturally to him. No extreme violence, no messy shootings or hacking or throttling. Just the right amount of poison, administered with skill and discretion.

A gentle, civilized sort of person, was Mr Jones. He collected butterflies and arranged them systematically in glass cases. His ether bottle was quick and painless. He never stuck pins into the beautiful creatures.

Have you ever heard of the Agra Double Murder? It happened, of course, a great many years ago, when Agra was a far-flung outpost of the British Empire. In those days, William Jones was a male nurse in one of the city's hospitals. The patients—especially terminal cases—spoke highly of the care and consideration he showed them. While most nurses, both male and female, preferred to attend to the more hopeful cases, Nurse William was always prepared to stand duty over a dying patient.

He felt a certain empathy for the dying. He liked to see them on their way. It was just his good nature, of course.

On a visit to nearby Meerut, he met and fell in love with Mrs Browning, the wife of the local stationmaster. Impassioned love letters were soon putting a strain on the Agra–Meerut postal service. The envelopes grew heavier—not so much because the letters were growing longer but because they contained little packets of a powdery white substance, accompanied by detailed instructions as to its correct administration.

Mr Browning, an unassuming and trustful man—one of the world's born losers, in fact—was not the sort to read his wife's correspondence. Even when he was seized by frequent attacks of colic, he put them down to an impure water supply. He recovered from one bout of vomiting and diarrhoea only to be racked by another.

He was hospitalized on a diagnosis of gastroenteritis. And, thus freed from his wife's ministrations, soon got better. But on returning home and drinking a glass of nimbu pani brought to him by the solicitous Mrs Browning, he had a relapse from which he did not recover.

Those were the days when deaths from cholera and related diseases were only too common in India and death certificates were easier to obtain than dog licences.

After a short interval of mourning (it was the hot weather and you couldn't wear black for long), Mrs Browning moved to Agra, where she rented a house next door to William Jones.

I forgot to mention that Mr Jones was also married. His wife was an insignificant creature, no match for a genius like William. Before the hot weather was over, the dreaded cholera had taken her too. The way was clear for the lovers to unite in holy matrimony.

But Dame Gossip lived in Agra, too, and it was not long before tongues were wagging and anonymous letters were being received by the superintendent of police. Inquiries were instituted. Like most infatuated lovers, Mrs Browning had hung on to her beloved's letters and billet-doux, and these soon came to light. The silly woman had kept them in a box beneath her bed.

Exhumations were ordered in both Agra and Meerut. Arsenic keeps well, even in the hottest of weather, and there was no dearth of it in the remains of both victims.

Mr Jones and Mrs Browning were arrested and charged with murder.

'Is Uncle Bill really a murderer?' I asked from the drawing-room sofa in my grandmother's house in Dehra. (It's time I told you that William Jones was my uncle, my mother's half-brother.)

I was eight or nine at the time. Uncle Bill had spent the previous summer with us in Dehra and had stuffed me with bazaar sweets and pastries, all of which I had consumed without suffering any ill effects.

'Who told you that about Uncle Bill?' asked Grandmother.

'I heard it in school. All the boys are asking me the same question—"Is your uncle a murderer?" They say he poisoned both his wives.'

'He had only one wife,' snapped Aunt Mabel.

'Did he poison her?'

'No, of course not. How can you say such a thing!'

'Then why is Uncle Bill in gaol?'

'Who says he's in gaol?'

'The boys at school. They heard it from their parents. Uncle Bill is to go on trial in the Agra fort.'

There was a pregnant silence in the drawing room, then Aunt Mabel burst out: 'It was all that awful woman's fault.'

'Do you mean Mrs Browning?' asked Grandmother.

'Yes, of course. She must have put him up to it. Bill couldn't have thought of anything so—so diabolical!'

'But he sent her the powders, dear. And don't forget—Mrs Browning has since . . .'

Grandmother stopped in mid-sentence, and both she and Aunt Mabel glanced surreptitiously at me.

'Committed suicide,' I filled in. 'There were still some powders with her.'

Aunt Mabel's eyes rolled heavenwards. 'This boy is impossible. I don't know what he will be like when he grows up.'

'At least I won't be like Uncle Bill,' I said. 'Fancy poisoning people! If I kill anyone, it will be in a fair fight. I suppose they'll hang Uncle?'

'Oh, I hope not!'

Grandmother was silent. Uncle Bill was her stepson but she did have a soft spot for him. Aunt Mabel, his sister, thought he was wonderful. I had always considered him to be a bit soft but had to admit that he was generous. I tried to imagine him dangling at the end of a hangman's rope, but somehow he didn't fit the picture.

As things turned out, he didn't hang. White people in India seldom got the death sentence, although the hangman was pretty busy disposing of dacoits and political terrorists. Uncle Bill was given a life sentence and settled down to a sedentary job in the prison library at Naini, near Allahabad. His gifts as a male nurse went unappreciated. They did not trust him in the hospital.

He was released after seven or eight years, shortly after the country became an independent republic. He came out of gaol to find that the British were leaving, either for England or the remaining colonies. Grandmother was dead. Aunt Mabel and her husband had settled in South Africa. Uncle Bill realized that there was little future for him in India and followed his sister out to Johannesburg. I was in my last year at boarding school. After my father's death my mother had married an Indian, and now my future lay in India.

I did not see Uncle Bill after his release from prison and no one dreamt that he would ever turn up again in India.

In fact, fifteen years were to pass before he came back, and by then I was in my early thirties, the author of a book that had become something of a bestseller. The previous fifteen years had been a struggle—the sort of struggle that every young freelance writer experiences—but at last, the hard work was paying off and the royalties were beginning to come in.

I was living in a small cottage on the outskirts of the hill station of Fosterganj, working on another book, when I received an unexpected visitor.

He was a thin, stooped, grey-haired man in his late fifties, with a straggling moustache and discoloured teeth. He looked feeble and harmless but for his eyes, which were a pale, cold, blue. There was something slightly familiar about him.

'Don't you remember me?' he asked. 'Not that I really expect you to, after all these years . . .'

'Wait a minute. Did you teach me at school?'

'No—but you're getting warm.' He put his suitcase down and I glimpsed his name on the airlines label. I looked up in astonishment. 'You're not—you couldn't be . . .'

'Your Uncle Bill,' he said with a grin and extended his hand. 'None other!' And he sauntered into the house.

I must admit that I had mixed feelings about his arrival. While I had never felt any dislike for him, I hadn't exactly approved of what he had done. Poisoning, I felt, was a particularly reprehensible way of getting rid of inconvenient people. Not that I could think of any commendable ways of getting rid of them! Still, it had happened a long time ago, he'd been punished, and presumably he was a reformed character.

'And what have you been doing all these years?' he asked me, easing himself into the only comfortable chair in the room.

'Oh, just writing,' I said.

'Yes, I heard about your last book. It's quite a success, isn't it?'

'It's doing quite well. Have you read it?'

'I don't do much reading.'

'And what have you been doing all these years, Uncle Bill?'

'Oh, knocking about here and there. Worked for a soft-drink company for some time. And then with a drug firm. My knowledge of chemicals was useful.'

'Weren't you with Aunt Mabel in South Africa?'

'I saw quite a lot of her until she died a couple of years ago. Didn't you know?'

'No. I've been out of touch with relatives.' I hoped he'd take that as a hint. 'And what about her husband?'

'Died too, not long after. Not many of us left, my boy. That's why, when I saw something about you in the papers, I thought—why not go and see my only nephew again?'

'You're welcome to stay a few days,' I said quickly. 'Then I have to go to Bombay.' (This was a lie but I did not relish the prospect of looking after Uncle Bill for the rest of his days.)

'Oh, I won't be staying long,' he said. 'I've got a bit of money put by in Johannesburg. It's just that—so far as I know—you're my only living relative, and I thought it would be nice to see you again.'

Feeling relieved, I set about trying to make Uncle Bill as comfortable as possible. I gave him my bedroom and turned the window seat into a bed for myself. I was a hopeless cook but, using all my ingenuity, I scrambled some eggs for supper. He waved aside my apologies. He'd always been a frugal eater, he said. Eight years in gaol had given him a cast-iron stomach.

He did not get in my way but left me to my writing and my lonely walks. He seemed content to sit in the spring sunshine and smoke his pipe.

It was during our third evening together that he said, 'Oh, I almost forgot. There's a bottle of sherry in my suitcase. I brought it especially for you.'

'That was very thoughtful of you, Uncle Bill. How did you know I was fond of sherry?'

'Just my intuition. You do like it, don't you?'

'There's nothing like a good sherry.'

He went to his bedroom and came back with an unopened bottle of South African sherry.

'Now you just relax near the fire,' he said agreeably. 'I'll open the bottle and fetch glasses.'

He went to the kitchen while I remained near the electric fire, flipping through some journals. It seemed to me that Uncle Bill was taking rather a long time. Intuition must be a family trait because it came to me quite suddenly—the thought that Uncle Bill might be intending to poison me.

After all, I thought, here he is, after nearly fifteen years, apparently for purely sentimental reasons. But I had just published a bestseller. And I was his nearest relative. If I were to die, Uncle Bill could lay claim to my estate and probably live comfortably on my royalties for the next five or six years!

What had really happened to Aunt Mabel and her husband, I wondered. And where did Uncle Bill get the money for an air ticket to India?

Before I could ask myself any more questions, he reappeared with the glasses on a tray. He set the tray on a small table that stood between us. The glasses had been filled. The sherry sparkled.

I stared at the glass nearest me, trying to make out if the liquid in it was cloudier than that in the other glass. But there appeared to be no difference.

I decided I would not take any chances. It was a round tray, made of smooth Kashmiri walnut wood. I turned it round with my index finger, so that the glasses changed places.

'Why did you do that?' asked Uncle Bill.

'It's a custom in these parts. You turn the tray with the sun, a complete revolution. It brings good luck.'

Uncle Bill looked thoughtful for a few moments, then said, 'Well, let's have some more luck,' and turned the tray round again.

'Now you've spoilt it,' I said. 'You're not supposed to keep revolving it! That's bad luck. I'll have to turn it about again to cancel out the bad luck.'

The tray swung round once more and Uncle Bill had the glass that was meant for me.

'Cheers!' I said and drank from my glass.

It was good sherry.

Uncle Bill hesitated. Then he shrugged, said 'Cheers' and drained his glass quickly.

But he did not offer to fill the glasses again.

Early next morning, he was taken violently ill. I heard him retching in his room and I got up and went to see if there was anything I could do. He was groaning, his head hanging over the side of the bed. I brought him a basin and a jug of water.

'Would you like me to fetch a doctor?' I asked.

He shook his head. 'No, I'll be all right. It must be something I ate.'

'It's probably the water. It's not too good at this time of the year. Many people come down with gastric trouble during their first few days in Fosterganj.'

'Ah, that must be it,' he said, and doubled up as a fresh spasm of pain and nausea swept over him.

He was better by evening—whatever had gone into the glass must have been by way of the preliminary dose, and a day later he was well enough to pack his suitcase and announce his departure. The climate of Fosterganj did not agree with him, he told me.

Just before he left, I said, 'Tell me, Uncle, why did you drink it?'

'Drink what? The water?'

'No, the glass of sherry into which you'd slipped one of your famous powders.'

He gaped at me, then gave a nervous, whinnying laugh. 'You will have your little joke, won't you?'

'No, I mean it,' I said. 'Why did you drink the stuff? It was meant for me, of course.'

He looked down at his shoes, then gave a little shrug and turned away.

'In the circumstances,' he said, 'it seemed the only decent thing to do.'

I'll say this for Uncle Bill: he was always the perfect gentleman.

LISTEN TO THE WIND

March is probably the most uncomfortable month in the hills. The rain is cold, often accompanied by sleet and hail, and the wind from the north comes tearing down the mountain passes with tremendous force. Those few people who pass the winter in the hill station remain close to their fires. If they can't afford fires, they get into bed.

I found old Miss Mackenzie tucked up in bed with three hot-water bottles for company. I took the bedroom's single easy chair, and for some time Miss Mackenzie and I listened to the thunder and watched the play of lightning. The rain made a tremendous noise on the corrugated tin roof, and we had to raise our voices in order to be heard. The hills looked blurred and smudgy when seen through the rain-spattered windows. The wind battered at the doors and rushed round the cottage, determined to make an entry; it slipped down the chimney, but stuck there, choking and gurgling and protesting helplessly.

'There's a ghost in your chimney and he can't get out,' I said.

'Then let him stay there,' said Miss Mackenzie.

A vivid flash of lightning lit up the opposite hill, showing me for a moment a pile of ruins which I never knew was there.

'You're looking at Burnt Hill,' said Miss Mackenzie. 'It always gets the lightning when there's a storm.'

'Possibly there are iron deposits in the rocks,' I said.

'I wouldn't know. But it's the reason why no one ever lived there for long. Almost every dwelling that was put up was struck by lightning and burnt down.'

'I thought I saw some ruins just now.'

'Nothing but rubble. When they were first settling in the hills, they chose that spot. Later they moved to the site where the town now stands. Burnt Hill was left to the deer and the leopards and the monkeys—and to its ghosts, of course . . .'

'Oh, so it's haunted, too.'

'So they say. On evenings such as these. But you don't believe in ghosts, do you?'

'No. Do you?'

'No. But you'll understand why they say the hill is haunted when you hear its story. Listen.'

I listened, but at first I could hear nothing but the wind and the rain. Then Miss Mackenzie's clear voice rose above the sound of the elements, and I heard her saying, '. . . it's really the old story of ill-starred lovers, only it's true.

'I'd met Robert at his parents' house some weeks before the tragedy took place. He was eighteen, tall and fresh-looking, and full of manhood. He'd been born out here, but his parents were hoping to return to England when Robert's father retired. His father was a magistrate, I think—but that hasn't any bearing on the story.

'Their plans didn't work out the way they'd expected. You see, Robert fell in love. Not with an English girl, mind you, but with a hill girl, the daughter of a landholder from the village behind Burnt Hill. Even today it would be unconventional. Twenty-five years ago, it was almost unheard of! Robert liked walking, and he was hiking through the forest when he saw, or rather heard, her. It was said later that he fell in love with her voice. She was singing, and the song—low and sweet and strange to his ears—struck him to the heart. When he caught sight of the girl's face, he was not disappointed. She was young and beautiful. She saw him and returned his awestruck gaze with a brief, fleeting smile.

'Robert, in his impetuousness, made inquiries at the village, located the girl's father, and without much ado, asked for her hand in marriage. He probably thought that a sahib would not be refused such a request. At the same time, it was really quite gallant on his part, because any other young man might simply have ravished the girl in the forest. But Robert was in love and, therefore, completely irrational in his behaviour.

'Of course, the girl's father would have nothing to do with the proposal. He was a Brahmin, and he wasn't going to have the good name of his family ruined by marrying off his only daughter to a foreigner. Robert did not argue with the father; nor did he say anything to his own parents, because he knew their reaction would be one of shock and dismay. They would do everything in their power to put an end to his madness.

'But Robert continued to visit the forest—you see it there, that heavy patch of oak and pine—and he often came across the girl, for she would be gathering fodder or fuel. She did not seem to resent his attentions, and, as Robert knew something of the language, he was soon able to convey his feelings to her. The girl must at first have been rather alarmed, but the boy's sincerity broke down her reserve. After all, she was young too—young enough to fall in love with a devoted swain, without thinking too much of his background. She knew her father would never agree to a marriage—and he knew his parents would prevent anything like that happening. So they planned to run away together. Romantic, isn't it? But it did happen. Only they did not live happily ever after.'

'Did their parents come after them?'

'No. They had agreed to meet one night in the ruined building on Burnt Hill—the ruin you saw just now; it hasn't changed much, except that there was a bit of roof to it then. They left their homes and made their way to the hill without any difficulty. After meeting, they planned to take the little path that followed the course of a stream, until it reached the plains. After that—but who knows what they had planned, what dreams of the future they had conjured up? The storm broke soon after they'd reached the ruins. They took shelter under the dripping ceiling. It was a storm just like this one—a high wind and great torrents of rain and hail, and the lightning flitting about and crashing down almost every minute. They must have been soaked, huddled together in a corner of that crumbling building, when lightning struck. No one knows at what time it happened. But next morning, their charred bodies were found on the worn, yellow stones of the old building.'

Miss Mackenzie stopped speaking, and I noticed that the thunder had grown distant and the rain had lessened; but the chimney was still coughing and clearing its throat.

'That is true, every word of it,' said Miss Mackenzie. 'But as to Burnt Hill being haunted, that's another matter. I've no experience of ghosts.'

'Anyway, you need a fire to keep them out of the chimney,' I said, getting up to go. I had my raincoat and umbrella, and my own cottage was not far away.

Next morning, when I took the steep path up to Burnt Hill, the sky was clear, and though there was still a stiff wind, it was no longer menacing. An hour's climb brought me to the old ruin—now nothing but a heap of stones, as Miss Mackenzie had said. Part of a wall was left, and the corner of a fireplace. Grass and weeds had grown up through the floor, and primroses and wild saxifrage flowered amongst the rubble.

Where had they sheltered, I wondered, as the wind tore at them and fire fell from the sky.

I touched the cold stones, half expecting to find in them some traces of the warmth of human contact. I listened, waiting for some ancient echo, some returning wave of sound, that would bring me nearer to the spirits of the dead lovers; but there was only the wind coughing in the lovely pines.

I thought I heard voices in the wind; and perhaps I did. For isn't the wind the voice of the undying dead?

THE LATE-NIGHT SHOW

According to the crime novels I used to read, there are four principal reasons for committing murder:

1. Money
2. Property
3. Revenge
4. Insanity, temporary or otherwise

In that order of priority.

But according to the crime movies I used to see, the priorities were a little different:

1. Passion (hate/jealousy)
2. Insanity (serial killing)
3. Money (bank hold-ups)
4. Espionage

Having grown up on crime fiction (both in literature and on film), I think my assessments are not far off the mark. When I put it to my friend Inspector Keemat Lal a few years ago, he said 50 per cent of murders were the result of greed—for money, property or another person's possessions. He was right, of course, but something as mundane as that doesn't make for great films or novels.

In the year I finished school, I was still staying with my mother in the old Green's Hotel in Dehradun. Just across the road was the Odeon, a small cinema that showed English and American films. Every winter, during the school holidays, I had been a regular picture-goer. Now that I had finished school, I was still a patron of the cinema, but preferred going to the night shows, from nine-thirty to twelve. At night, the hall was usually half-empty, and the usher-cum-ticket-collector, who had become a friend of mine, would let me in without a ticket—provided I occupied one of the cheaper seats. As pocket money was in short supply (my mother's salary was both poor and irregular), I readily accepted my friend's assistance. In this way, I saw almost every Hollywood or British film made around that period.

Just as much of my reading was centred around Agatha Christie, Ellery Queen and Edgar Wallace, so did my taste in films veer towards the slick thrillers in which stars such as James Cagney, Humphrey Bogart and Edward G. Robinson portrayed various colourful characters from the underworld. Back then, I remember how strange it felt, watching these actors transition from their roles as gangsters or outlaws to portraying detective heroes (as Bogart did in *The Maltese Falcon*) or even appearing in musicals (like Cagney in *Yankee Doodle Dandy*).

If today I have an almost encyclopedic knowledge of films made in the 1940s and 1950s, it is due largely to my usher friend who allowed me into the Odeon night after night, putting his job at some risk in doing so. I reciprocated by bringing him the occasional bottle of beer from the Green's bar. The barman, too, was a friend of mine.

There were other regulars who came to the night shows—salesmen, shopkeepers, waiters, those who did not get much time off during the day. And some old characters too—like the retired postmaster who never missed a film but always fell asleep after a couple of reels and whose snoring drowned out the sound from the projection room; or the hunchback who always sat in the front row because he couldn't see anything from the back; or the man who drank endless cups of tea throughout the show. Mostly menfolk. Women seldom came to the night show, unless escorted by husbands or family.

One regular always intrigued me. He was a man in his thirties who sat through the show without ever removing his hat. Presumably he was bald and felt the cold draught that ran through the hall whenever one of the doors was opened. In January the hall could be cold. He wore an overcoat too, which also served as a receptacle for packets of chana which he munched assiduously during the film. Those were the days before fast foods of various descriptions took over. You had a choice between peanuts and chana. And apart from tea, there was a crimson-coloured cold drink called Vimto, which had a raspberry flavour. The gentleman with the hat always drank Vimto.

There was no social intercourse during the film. Either you saw the picture or you left the hall. The hatted gentleman almost always took the same seat, not far from one of the exit doors. Occasionally he would have a companion, but not for long. Mr Hat watched the film in its entirety, but the companions came and went. Sometimes he would offer them something from the folds of his overcoat. They would pocket the offering and leave after a few minutes.

One night, there was a little more activity than usual in the row where Mr Hat was sitting. He came with a companion, who left after a few minutes. A little later he was joined by another person. I did not pay much attention to them. I was engrossed in *The Third Man*, Anton Karas's haunting zither music building up to the chase in the sewers of Vienna, with

Joseph Cotten hunting down his black-marketeer friend, Orson Welles. Cotten, not Welles, was my favourite actor.

The activity around Mr Hat was something of a distraction, and one or two in the hall shouted to them to shut up or go home. One of his companions, a tall individual, got up suddenly and walked towards the exit. He passed in front of me. And when he pushed open the door, the light from the foyer fell on his face and I caught a glimpse of narrow eyes, a large hooked nose and a jutting chin. Then the door closed and I was back in the world of post-war Vienna. Ten minutes later, the film was over and the lights came on. We began moving slowly out of the theatre—reluctantly, as it was freezing outside.

Mr Hat hadn't moved. He was hunched forward, his hat tilted over his head. I thought he'd fallen asleep. Curious as ever, I took a few steps down the central aisle and looked down at him. At first I thought he'd spilled a bottle of Vimto over his unbuttoned coat and shirt front. Then I realized that it was blood, not Vimto, that had gushed out of his torn and still bleeding throat. I cried out, and my usher friend came running. Then the manager. Then the tea-stall owner. Then those who were still in the hall.

'His throat's been cut,' said someone. 'He's dead or dying.'

And by the time a policeman and a doctor arrived, Mr Hat's lifeblood had seeped away.

* * *

It was two or three weeks before I visited the Odeon again, and then, too, only for a matinee.

'No more night shows,' said my mother. 'You must be in the hotel by nine, and preferably in your bed.'

'But it had nothing to do with me,' I protested. 'He was just another filmgoer.'

'No ordinary filmgoer gets stabbed to death in the middle of a picture. Wasn't someone with him?'

'Sometimes. I didn't really notice.'

But I had noticed the tall, hawk-nosed man who had left before the show ended. I would recognize him again. But I did not tell my mother this.

With nothing much to do late in the evening, I began hanging around the Green's Hotel bar, where the bartender, Melaram, often chatted to me if he wasn't too busy. I sat by myself in a corner of the large, dimly lit room, watching the customers and sipping a shandy. I would have preferred a beer, but my mother had given Melaram instructions to serve me with nothing stronger than shandy.

'A pity you can't go to the Odeon any more,' he said sympathetically. 'Not at night, anyway. Why don't you go to the afternoon shows?'

'The free pass was only for the night shows,' I told him. 'The hall is practically empty at night.'

'Not surprising, with people getting murdered in their seats.'

'It only happened once.'

'True . . . So how would you like to see a Hindi movie? You can come with me. We'll go to the Filmistan. Your mother won't mind.'

So Melaram took me to see an extravaganza called *Alibaba aur 40 Chor*, which was the sort of film Melaram enjoyed. All I remember is that it had a nifty little heroine called Shakeela, who was easy on the eye.

The following week we saw another film, and this time we were accompanied by my friend Sitaram, one of the room boys. We sat in the cheaper seats and clapped with the tonga wallahs and labourers whenever the dashing hero (Dilip Kumar) rescued the coy heroine (Nalini Jaywant) from the menacing villain (Pran, as usual).

As we left the cinema and were about to cross the road, I thought I saw the man who had passed me in the Odeon the night Mr Hat had been killed. He looked at me, hesitated for a moment, and then passed on. Had he recognized me?

'Someone you know?' asked Melaram at my side.

'That fellow who just passed,' I said. 'I think he was with the man who got killed that night.'

'Well, better keep quiet about it,' said Melaram. 'I think he's from one of the drug gangs. If you see him again, don't let him think you recognize him.'

* * *

To my surprise, the next time I saw him was in the Green's bar. He strode in, as though looking for someone, then shrugged, sat down on a bar stool and ordered a beer. I was in my dark corner, and he probably would not have noticed me just then, had I not got up and left the room by the service door. I felt his eyes on me. I thought it best not to hang around, so went to my room (my mother had allowed me to use one of the smaller hotel rooms), locked the door, switched on the bed light and immersed myself in *Wuthering Heights*.

It was the right sort of book for such a night. Outside, a storm had broken, thunder rolled across the heavens, and the rain came rattling down on the corrugated tin roof. I read for an hour or two, then looked at my watch—given to me recently for having passed out of school. It was only eleven o'clock. I switched off the light and tried to sleep. Presently, the thunder grew more distant, the rain lessened. A breeze sprang up, and a bunch of bougainvillea kept tapping against the windowpanes.

And then, someone was tapping on my door.

A light tap to begin with, and then louder, more insistent.

'Who's there?' I called, but no one answered.

Had it been the nightwatchman, or Sitaram at a loose end, they would have said something. Perhaps Sitaram up to tricks?

'Go to bed,' I called out. 'I'm sleepy.'

No answer. But after a little while, more knocking. Then silence. Then footsteps receding.

I switched on my bedside radio and lay awake, listening to popular songs that held no special meaning for me. But at least the radio was company. Finally I fell asleep, the music still playing.

It must have been towards dawn that I woke again. The radio was still on, but the station had gone off the air and there was a lot of static coming over the airwaves. I switched it off.

That tapping again. But now it came from the window, not the door.

I got up on my knees and drew aside the window curtain. There was a face pressed against the glass. An outside light fell upon it and made it look more hideous than it really was. The slit eyes, hooked nose and wide, sensual mouth seemed more sinister than ever. Boris Karloff as Frankenstein couldn't have been more frightening.

The apparition smiled at me, and I let the curtain fall.

And then I did a foolish thing. I leapt out of bed, opened my door and ran barefoot down the corridor, calling for Sitaram, Melaram, the chowkidar, anyone!

But no one came. It was the hour before dawn, and no one stirred.

I ran out on to the back veranda, and he was waiting there—Hook Nose was waiting. In his right hand he held a kukri, its blade shining in the lamplight.

I turned and ran into the wilderness behind the hotel. A path ran down the slope and into a tangle of jungle. I knew it well. He was running after me, crashing clumsily through the lantana,

but I was faster than him, and I kept running until I came to an abandoned cowshed that stood at the edge of the jungle.

I did not enter it. He would have caught me there. Instead, I crouched behind some bushes—and waited.

He was not long in coming. He stopped in front of the open door—the shed's only door—then stepped inside. I could hear him stumbling around in the dark.

I crept up to the door, pulled it shut and slid the bolt in. It was an old door, but strong, made of deodar wood. There were no windows in the shed, just a small slit high up on the wall. Mr Hook Nose would have to break the door down in order to get out. He'd need an axe to do that. Already he was hammering away with his fists and cursing.

I left him to it, and returned to the hotel.

Dawn was breaking. A cock crowed near the kitchen outhouse, while an early riser emerged from his room, yelling for his morning tea.

* * *

I went to Bareilly to spend a month with one of my aunts. There were no bookshops in Bareilly, and no English cinema, and I was soon restless and eager to return to Dehradun.

When I got down at the station, Sitaram was there to meet me.

He told me that Melaram had gone to a new and bigger hotel, and that Green's had a new but inexperienced bartender. He also brought me up to date on all the films that were running in town.

Was it fear, curiosity, a morbid fascination that took me down to the old cowshed that very afternoon? Somehow I had to know if Hook Nose had escaped, or if he was still there, now a bag of bones!

I had lunch with my mother, then said I was going for a walk—it was a bracing February afternoon in the Doon—and took the jungle path down to the shed.

It was still locked. Dared I open that door? Would the revenant of Hook Nose come rushing out at me? Worse still, would I find his remains putrefying in the dust?

Well, I had to find out.

I opened the door and stepped inside.

It was so dark I could hardly see anything. In the stale air, there was the smell of muskrats and rotting vegetation. But nothing that I would describe as a human smell.

I looked around. Toadstools grew on the floor. There was a pile of wood in one corner. A large grey rat ran out from under the woodpile and out through the open door. No sign of Hook Nose anywhere. Either he'd escaped on his own or someone had set him free. I felt relieved, but also apprehensive. What if he came looking for me again?

That evening, as I emerged from my room, Sitaram took me by the hand and said, 'Come on, the bar's open. I'll get you a beer. No customers as yet.'

I was still a year under the legal limit for drinking in a bar, but that didn't stop me from perching on a bar stool while Sitaram went in search of something for me to eat.

The bartender had his back to me. When he turned, a bottle of Golden Eagle in his hands, I received the shock of my life. It was Hook Nose!

I almost fell off my stool. My first impulse was to get up and run. But his face was expressionless. All he did was open the bottle and top up a glass with beer, and place it before me. Was it possible that he did not recognize me?

Sitaram was beckoning me to a table in a dark alcove.

I hurried towards him.

'Who's the new bartender?' I asked urgently.

'Don't know his name,' said Sitaram, speaking rapidly in Hindustani. 'I don't think he knows it himself. Your mother felt sorry for him and gave him the job. Somehow he'd got locked into that old shed behind the hotel. Must have been there for several days before he was found, just by chance, when we went there for some firewood—he'd had nothing to eat and drink, and he'd hurt his head trying to get out. Lost his memory. Couldn't remember a thing. Had nowhere to go. So your mother gave him a job. He goes about in a bit of a daze, but he's all right for serving drinks. Perhaps he'll start remembering things one of these days . . . Why are you looking worried? It's no concern of yours. Come on, finish your beer and we'll go to the pictures. I've got the night off. There's a new film with Nimmi in it. You like her, don't you?'

WHEN DARKNESS FALLS

Markham had, for many years, lived alone in a small room adjoining the disused cellars of the old Empire Hotel in one of our hill stations. His Army pension gave him enough money to pay for his room rent and his basic needs, but he shunned the outside world—by daylight, anyway—partly because of a natural reticence and partly because he wasn't very nice to look at.

While Markham was serving in Burma during the War, a shell had exploded near his dugout, tearing away most of his face. Plastic surgery was then in its infancy, and although the doctors had done their best, even going to the extent of giving Markham a false nose, his features were permanently ravaged. On the few occasions that he had walked abroad by day, he had been mistaken for someone in the final stages of leprosy and been given a wide berth.

He had been given the basement room by the hotel's elderly estate manager, Negi, who had known Markham in the years before the War, when Negi was just a room boy. Markham had himself been a youthful assistant manager at the time, and he had helped the eager young Negi advance from room boy to bartender to office clerk. When Markham took up a wartime commission, Negi rose even further. Now Markham was well into his late sixties, with Negi not very far behind. After a post-War, post-Independence slump, the hill station was thriving again; but both Negi and Markham belonged to another era, another time and place. So did the old hotel, now going to seed, but clinging to its name and surviving on its reputation.

'We're dead, but we won't lie down,' joked Markham, but he didn't find it very funny.

Day after day, alone in the stark simplicity of his room, there was little he could do except read or listen to his short-wave transistor radio; but he would emerge at night to prowl about the vast hotel grounds and occasionally take a midnight stroll along the deserted Mall.

During these forays into the outer world, he wore an old felt hat, which hid part of his face. He had tried wearing a mask, but that had been even more frightening for those who saw it, especially under a street lamp. A couple of honeymooners, walking back to the hotel late at night, had come face-to-face with Markham and had fled the hill station the next day. Dogs did not like the mask, either. They set up a furious barking at Markham's approach, stopping only when he removed the mask; they did not seem to mind his face. A policeman returning home late had accosted Markham, suspecting him of being a burglar, and snatched off the mask. Markham, sans nose, jaw and one eye, had smiled a crooked smile, and the policeman had taken to his heels. Thieves and goondas he could handle; not ghostly apparitions straight out of hell.

Apart from Negi, only a few knew of Markham's existence. These were the lower-paid employees who had grown used to him over the years, as one gets used to a lame dog or a crippled cow. The gardener, the sweeper, the dhobi, the night chowkidar, all knew him as a sort of presence. They did not look at him. A man with one eye is said to have the evil eye, and one baleful glance from Markham's single eye was enough to upset anyone with a superstitious nature. He had no problems with the menial staff, and he wisely kept away from the hotel lobby, bar, dining room and corridors—he did not want to frighten the customers away; that would have spelt an end to his own liberty. The owner, who was away most of the time, did not know of his existence; nor did his wife, who lived in the east wing of the hotel, where Markham had never ventured.

The hotel covered a vast area, which included several unused buildings and decaying outhouses. There was a Beer Garden, no longer frequented, overgrown with weeds and untamed shrubbery. There were tennis courts, rarely used; a squash court, inhabited by a family of goats; a children's playground with a broken see-saw; a ballroom which hadn't seen a ball in fifty years; cellars which were never opened; and a billiard room, said to be haunted.

As his name implied, Markham's forebears were English, with a bit of Allahabad thrown in. It was said that he was related to Kipling on his mother's side; but he never made this claim himself. He had fair hair and one grey-blue eye. The other, of course, was missing.

His artificial nose could be removed whenever he wished, and as he found it a little uncomfortable, he usually took it off when he was alone in his room. It rested on his bedside table, staring at the ceiling. Over the years, it had acquired a character of its own and those (like Negi) who had seen it looked upon it with a certain amount of awe. Markham avoided looking at himself in the mirror, but sometimes he had to shave one side of his face, which included a few surviving teeth; there was a gaping hole in his left cheek. And after all these years, it still looked raw.

* * *

When it was past midnight, Markham emerged from his lair and prowled the grounds of the old hotel. They belonged to him, really, as no one else patrolled them at that hour—not even the night chowkidar, who was usually to be found asleep on a tattered sofa outside the lounge.

Wearing his old hat and cape, Markham did his rounds.

He was a ghostly figure, no doubt, and the few who had glimpsed him in those late hours had taken him for a supernatural visitor. In this way, the hotel had acquired a reputation for being haunted. Some guests liked the idea of having a resident ghost; others stayed away.

On this particular night, Markham was more restless than usual, more discontented with himself in particular and with the world in general; he wanted a little change—and who wouldn't, in similar circumstances?

He had promised Negi that he would avoid the interior of the hotel as far as possible; but it was midsummer, the days were warm and languid, the nights cool and balmy, and he felt like being in the proximity of other humans even if he could not socialize with them.

And so, late at night, he slipped out of the passage to his cellar room and ascended the steps that led to the old banquet hall, now just a huge dining room. A single light was burning at the end of the hall. Beneath it stood an old piano.

Markham lifted the lid and ran his fingers over the keys. He could still pick out a tune, although it had been many years since he had played for anyone or even for himself. Now at least he could indulge himself a little. An old song came back to him and he played it softly, hesitantly, recalling a few words:

> But it's a long, long time, from May to December,
> And the days grow short when we reach September . . .

He couldn't remember all the words, so he just hummed a little as he played. Suddenly, something came down with a crash at the other end of the room. Markham looked up, startled. The hotel cat had knocked over a soup tureen that had been left on one of the tables. Seeing Markham's tall, shifting shadow on the wall, its hair stood on end. And with a long, low wail it fled the banquet room.

Markham left too, and made his way up the carpeted staircase to the first-floor corridor.

Not all the rooms were occupied. They seldom were, these days. He tried one or two doors, but they were locked. He walked to the end of the passage and tried the last door. It was open.

Assuming the room was unoccupied, he entered it quietly. The lights were off, but there was sufficient moonlight coming through the large bay window with its view of the mountains. Markham looked towards the large double bed and saw that it was occupied. A young couple lay there, fast asleep, wrapped in each other's arms. A touching sight! Markham smiled bitterly. It was over forty years since anyone had lain in his arms.

There were footsteps in the passage. Someone stood outside the closed door. Had Markham been seen prowling about the corridors? He moved swiftly to the window, unlatched it, and stepped quickly out on to the landing abutting the roof. Quietly he closed the window and moved away.

Outside, on the roof, he felt an overwhelming sense of freedom. No one would find him there. He wondered why he hadn't thought of the roof before. Being on it gave him a feeling of ownership. The hotel, and all who lived in it, belonged to him.

The lights from a few skylights, and the moon above, helped him to move unhindered over the sloping, corrugated old tin roof. He looked out at the mountains, striding away into the heavens. He felt at one with them.

The owner, Mr Khanna, was away on one of his extended trips abroad. Known to his friends as the, 'Playboy of the

Western World', he spent a great deal of his time and money in foreign capitals: London, Paris, New York, Amsterdam. Mr Khanna's wife had health problems (mostly in her mind) and seldom travelled, except to visit god-men and faith healers. At this point in time, she was suffering from insomnia, and was pacing about her room in her dressing gown, a loose-fitting garment that did little to conceal her overblown figure; for in spite of her many ailments, her appetite for everything on the menu card was undiminished. Right now she was looking for her sleeping tablets. Where on earth had she put them? They were not on her bedside table; not on the dressing table; not on the bathroom shelf. Perhaps they were in her handbag. She rummaged in a drawer, found and opened the bag, and extracted a strip of Valium. Pouring herself a glass of water from the bedside carafe, she tossed her head back, revealing several layers of chin. Before she could swallow the tablet, she saw a face at the skylight. Not really a face. Not a human face, that is. An empty eye socket, a wicked grin, and a nose that wasn't a nose, pressed flat against the glass.

Mrs Khanna sank to the floor and passed out. She had no need of the sleeping tablet that night.

* * *

For the next couple of days, Mrs Khanna was quite hysterical and spoke wildly of a wolf-man or Rakshas who was pursuing her. But no one—not even Negi—attributed the apparition to Markham, who had always avoided the guests' rooms.

The daylight hours, he passed in his cellar room, which received only a dapple of late-afternoon sunlight through a narrow aperture that passed for a window. For about ten minutes, the sun rested on a framed picture of Markham's mother, a severe-looking but handsome woman, who must have been in her forties when the picture was taken. His father, an Army captain, had been killed in the trenches at Mons during the First World War. His picture stood there, too; a dashing figure in uniform. Sometimes Markham wished that he, too, had died from his wounds; but he had been kept alive, and then he had stayed dead-alive all these years, a punishment, maybe, for sins and excesses committed in some former existence. Perhaps there was something in the theory or belief in karma, although he wished that things could even out a little more in this life—why did we have to wait for the next time around? Markham had read Emerson's essay on the law of compensation, but that didn't seem to work either. He had often thought of suicide as a way of cheating the fates that had made him, the child of handsome parents, no better than a hideous gargoyle; but he had thrust the thought aside, hoping (as most of us do) that things would change for the better.

His room was tidy—it had the bare necessities—and those pictures were the only mementos of a past he couldn't forget. He had his books, too, for he considered them necessities— the Greek philosophers, Epicurus, Epictetus, Marcus Aurelius, Seneca. When Seneca had nothing left to live for, he had cut his wrists in his bathtub and bled slowly to death. Not a bad way to go, thought Markham; except that he didn't have a bathtub, only a rusty iron bucket.

Food was left outside his door, as per instructions; sometimes fresh fruit and vegetables, sometimes a cooked meal. If there was a wedding banquet in the hotel, Negi would remember to send Markham some roast chicken or pilau. Markham looked forward to the marriage season, with its lavish wedding parties. He was a permanent, though unknown, wedding guest.

After discovering the freedom of the Empire's roof, Markham's nocturnal excursions seldom went beyond the hotel's sprawling estate. As sure-footed as when he was a soldier, he had no difficulty in scrambling over the decaying rooftops, moving along narrow window ledges, and leaping from one landing or balcony to another. It was late summer, and guests often left their windows open to enjoy the pine-scented breeze that drifted over the hillside. Markham was no voyeur, he was really too insular and subjective a person for that form of indulgence; nevertheless, he found it fascinating to observe people in their unguarded moments: how they preened in front of mirrors, or talked to themselves, or attended to their little vanities, or sang or scratched or made love (or tried to), or drank themselves into a stupor. There were many men (and a few women) who preferred drinking in their rooms to drinking in the bar—it was cheaper, and they could get drunk and stupid without making fools of themselves in public.

One of those who enjoyed a quiet tipple in her room was Mrs Khanna. A vodka with tomato juice was her favourite drink. Markham was watching her soak up her third Bloody Mary when the room telephone rang and Mrs Khanna, receiving some urgent message, left her room and went swaying down the corridor like a battleship of yore.

On an impulse, Markham slipped in through the open window and crossed the room to the table where the bottles were arranged. He felt like having a Bloody Mary himself. It had been years since he'd had one; not since that evening at New Delhi's Imperial, when he was on his first leave. Now, a little rum during the winter months was his only indulgence.

Taking a clean glass, he poured himself three fingers of vodka and drank it neat. He was about to pour himself another drink when Mrs Khanna entered the room. She stood frozen in her tracks. For there stood the creature of her previous nightmare, the half-face wolf-demon, helping himself to her vodka!

Mrs Khanna screamed. And screamed again.

Markham made a quick exit through the window and vanished into the night. But Mrs Khanna would not stop screaming—not until Negi, half the staff and several guests had entered the room to try and calm her down.

* * *

Commotion reigned for a couple of days. Doctors came and went. Policemen came and went. So did Mrs Khanna's palpitations. She insisted that the hotel be searched for the maniac who was in hiding somewhere, only emerging from his lair to single her out for attention. Negi kept the searchers away from the cellar, but he went down himself and confronted Markham.

'Mr Markham, sir, you must keep away from the rooms and the main hotel. Mrs Khanna is very upset. She's called in the police and she's having the hotel searched.'

'I'm sorry, Mr Negi. I did not mean to frighten anyone. It's just that I get restless down here.'

'If she finds out you're living here, you'll have to go. She gives the orders when Mr Khanna is away.'

'This is my only home. Where would I go?'

'I know, Mr Markham, I know. I understand. But do others? It unnerves them, coming upon you without any warning. Stories are going around . . . Business is bad enough without the hotel getting a reputation for strange goings-on. If you must go out at night, use the rear gate and stick to the forest path. Avoid the Mall Road. Times have changed, Mr Markham. There are no private places any more. If you have to leave, you will be in the public eye—and I know you don't want that . . .'

'No, I can't leave this place. I'll stick to my room. You've been good to me, Mr Negi.'

'That's all right. I'll see that you get what you need. Just keep out of sight.'

So Markham confined himself to his room for a week, two weeks, three, while the monsoon rains swept across the hills, and a clinging mist gave everything a musty, rotting smell. By mid-August, life in a hill station can become quite depressing for its residents. The absence of sunshine has something to do with it. Even strolling along the Mall is not much fun when a thin, cloying drizzle is drifting into your face. No wonder some take to drink. The hotel bar had a few more customers than usual, although the carpet stank of mildew and rats' urine.

Markham made friends with a shrew that used to visit his room. Shrews have poor eyesight and are easily caught and killed. But as they are supposed to bring good fortune, they were left alone by the hotel staff. Markham was grateful for a little company, and fed his shrew on biscuits and dry bread. It moved about his room quite freely and slept in the bottom drawer of his dressing table. Unlike the cat, it had no objection to Markham's face—or the lack of it.

Towards the end of August, when there was still no relief from the endless rain and cloying mist, Markham grew restless again. He made one brief, nocturnal visit to the park behind the hotel, and came back soaked to the skin. It seemed a pointless exercise, tramping through the long, leech-infested grass. What he really longed for was to touch that piano again. Bits of old music ran through his head. He wanted to pick out a few tunes on that cracked old instrument in the deserted ballroom.

The rain was thundering down on the corrugated tin roofs. There had been a power failure—common enough on nights like this—and most of the town, including the hotel, had been plunged into darkness. There was no need of mask or cape. No need for his false nose, either. Only in the occasional flash of lightning could you see his torn and ravaged countenance.

Markham slipped out of his room and made his way through the cellars beneath the ballroom. It was a veritable jungle down there. No longer used as a wine cellar, the complex was really a storeroom for old and rotting furniture, rusty old boilers from another age, broken garden urns, even a chipped and mutilated statue of Cupid. It had stood in the garden in former times; but recently the town municipal committee had objected to it as being un-Indian and obscene, and so it had been banished to the cellar.

That had been several years ago, and since then no one had been down into the cellars. It was Markham's shortcut to the living world above.

It had stopped raining, and a sliver of moon shone through the clouds. There were still no lights in the hotel. But Markham was used to darkness. He slipped into the ballroom and approached the old piano.

He sat there for half an hour, strumming out old tunes.

There was one old favourite that kept coming back to him, and he played it again and again, recalling the words as he went along.

Oh, pale dispenser of my joys and pains,
Holding the doors of Heaven and of Hell,
How the hot blood rushed wildly through the veins
Beneath your touch, until you waved farewell.

The words of Laurence Hope's Kashmiri love song took him back to happier times when life had seemed full of possibilities. And when he came to the end of the song, he felt his loss even more passionately:

Pale hands, pink-tipped, like lotus buds that float
On these cool waters where we used to dwell,
I would have rather felt you round my throat
crushing out life, than waving me farewell!

He had loved and been loved once. But that had been a long, long time ago. Pale hands he'd loved, beside the Shalimar . . .

He stopped playing. All was still.

Should he return to his room now, and keep his promise to Negi? But then again, no one was likely to be around on a night like this, reasoned Markham; and he had no intention of entering any of the rooms. Through the glass doors at the other end of the ballroom he could see a faint glow, as of a firefly in the darkness. He moved towards the light, as a moth to a flame. It was the chowkidar's lantern. He lay asleep on an old sofa, from which the stuffing was protruding.

Markham's was a normal mind handicapped by a physical abnormality. But how long can a mind remain normal in such circumstances?

Markham took the chowkidar's lamp and advanced into the lobby. Moth-eaten stags' heads stared down at him from the walls. They had been shot about a hundred years ago, when the hunting of animals had been in fashion. The taxidermist's art had given them a semblance of their former nobility; but time had taken its toll. A mounted panther's head had lost its glass eyes. Even so, thought Markham wryly, its head is in better shape than mine!

The door of the barroom opened to a gentle pressure. The bartender had been tippling on the quiet and had neglected to close the door properly. Markham placed the lamp on a table and looked up at the bottles arrayed in front of him. Some foreign wines, sherries and vermouth. Rum, gin and vodka. He'd never been much of a drinker; drink went to his head rather too quickly, he'd always known that. But the bottles certainly looked attractive, and he felt in need of some sustenance, so he poured himself a generous peg of whisky and drank it neat. A warm glow spread through his body. He felt a little better about himself. Life could be made tolerable if he had more frequent access to the bar!

Pacing about in her room on the floor above, Mrs Khanna heard a noise downstairs. She had always suspected the bartender, Ram Lal, of helping himself to liquor on the quiet. After ten o'clock, his gait was unsteady, and in the mornings, he often turned up rather groggy and unshaven. Well, she was going to catch him red-handed tonight!

Markham sat on a bar stool with his back to the swing doors. Mrs Khanna, entering on tiptoe, could only make out the outline of a man's figure pouring himself a drink.

The wind in the passage muffled the sound of Mrs Khanna's approach. And anyway, Markham's mind was far away, in the distant Shalimar Bagh where hands, pink-tipped, touched his lips and cheeks, his face yet undespoiled.

'Ram Lal!' hissed Mrs Khanna, intent on scaring the bartender out of his wits. 'Having a good time again?'

Markham was startled, but he did not lose his head. He did not turn immediately.

'I'm not Ram Lal, Mrs Khanna,' said Markham quietly. 'Just one of your guests. An old resident, in fact. You've seen me around before. My face was badly injured a long time ago. I'm not very nice to look at. But there's nothing to be afraid of. I'm quite normal, you know.'

Markham got up slowly. He held his cape up to his face and began moving slowly towards the swing doors. But Mrs Khanna was having none of it. She reached out and snatched at the cape. In the flickering lamplight, she stared into that dreadful face. She opened her mouth to scream.

But Markham did not want to hear her screams again. They shattered the stillness and beauty of the night. There was nothing beautiful about a woman's screams—especially Mrs Khanna's.

He reached out for his tormentor and grabbed her by the throat. He wanted to stop her screaming, that was all. But he had strong hands. Struggling, the pair of them knocked over a chair and fell against the table.

'Quite normal, Mrs Khanna,' he said, again and again, his voice ascending. 'I'm quite normal!'

Her legs slid down beneath a bar stool. Still he held on, squeezing, pressing. All those years of frustration were in that grip. Crushing out life and waving it farewell!

Involuntarily, she flung out an arm and knocked over the lamp. Markham released his grip; she fell heavily to the carpet. A rivulet of burning oil sped across the floor and set fire to the hem of her nightgown. But Mrs Khanna was now oblivious to what was happening. The flames took hold of a curtain and ran up towards the wooden ceiling.

Markham picked up a jug of water and threw it on the flames. It made no difference. Horrified, he dashed through the swing doors and called for help. The chowkidar stirred sluggishly and called out, '*Khabardar*! Who goes there?' He saw a red glow in the bar, rubbed his eyes in consternation and began looking for his lamp. He did not really need one. Bright flames were leaping out of the French windows.

'Fire!' shouted the chowkidar, and ran for help.

The old hotel, with its timbered floors and ceilings, oaken beams and staircases, mahogany and rosewood furniture, was a veritable tinderbox. By the time the chowkidar could summon help, the fire had spread to the dining room and was licking its way up the stairs to the first-floor rooms.

Markham had already ascended the staircase and was pounding on doors, shouting, 'Get up, get up! Fire below!'

He ran to the far end of the corridor, where Negi had his room, and pounded on the door with his fists until Negi woke up.

'The hotel's on fire!' shouted Markham, and ran back the way he had come. There was little more that he could do.

Some of the hotel staff were now rushing about with buckets of water, but the stairs and landing were ablaze, and those living on the first floor had to retreat to the servants' entrance, where a flight of stone steps led down to the tennis courts. Here they gathered, looking on in awe and consternation as the fire spread rapidly through the main building, showing itself at the windows as it went along. The small group on the tennis courts was soon joined by outsiders, for bad news spreads as fast as a good fire, and the townsfolk were not long in turning up.

Markham emerged on the roof, and stood there for some time, while the fire ran through the Empire Hotel, crackling vigorously and lighting up the sky. The people below spotted him on the roof, and waved and shouted to him to come down. Smoke billowed around him, and then he disappeared from view.

* * *

It was a fire to remember. The town hadn't seen anything like it since the Abbey School had gone up in flames forty years earlier, and only the older residents could remember that one. Negi and the hotel staff could only watch helplessly, as the fire raged through the old timbered building, consuming all that stood in its way. Everyone was out of the building, except Mrs Khanna, and as yet no one had any idea as to what had happened to her.

Towards morning it began raining heavily again, and this finally quenched the fire; but by then the buildings had been gutted, and the Empire Hotel, that had stood protectively over the town for over a hundred years, was no more.

Mrs Khanna's charred body was recovered from the ruins. A telegram was sent to Mr Khanna in Geneva, and phone calls were made to sundry relatives and insurance offices. Negi was very much in charge.

When the initial confusion was over, Negi remembered Markham and walked around to the rear of the gutted building and down the cellar steps. The basement and the cellar had escaped the worst of the fire, but they were still full of smoke. Negi found Markham's door open.

Markham was stretched out on his bed. The empty bottle of sleeping tablets on the bedside table told its own story; but it was more likely that he had suffocated from the smoke.

Markham's artificial nose lay on the dressing table. Negi picked it up and placed it on the dead man's poor face.

The hotel had gone, and with it Negi's livelihood. An old friend had gone, too. An era had passed. But Negi was the sort who liked to tidy up afterwards.

THE OVERCOAT

It was clear, frosty weather, and as the moon came up over the Himalayan peaks, I could see that patches of snow still lay on the roads of the hill station. I would have been quite happy in bed, with a book and a hot-water bottle at my side, but I'd promised the Kapadias that I'd go to their party, and I felt it would be churlish of me to stay away. I put on two sweaters, an old football scarf and an overcoat, and set off down the moonlit road.

It was a walk of just over a mile to the Kapadias' house, and I had covered about half the distance, when I saw a girl standing in the middle of the road.

She must have been sixteen or seventeen. She looked rather old-fashioned—long hair hanging to her waist, and a flouncy sequined dress, pink and lavender, that reminded me of the photos in my grandmother's family album. When I went closer, I noticed that she had lovely eyes and a winning smile.

'Good evening,' I said. 'It's a cold night to be out.'

'Are you going to the party?' she asked.

'That's right. And I can see from your lovely dress that you're going too. Come along, we're nearly there.'

She fell into step beside me, and we soon saw lights from the Kapadias' house shining brightly through the deodars. The girl told me her name was Julie. I hadn't seen her before, but I'd only been in the hill station a few months.

There was quite a crowd at the party, and no one seemed to know Julie. Everyone thought she was a friend of mine. I did not deny it. Obviously, she was someone who was feeling lonely and wanted to be friendly with people. And she was certainly enjoying herself. I did not see her do much eating or drinking, but she flitted from one group to another, talking, listening, laughing; and when the music began, she was dancing almost continuously, alone or with partners, it didn't matter which, she was completely wrapped up in the music.

It was almost midnight when I got up to go. I had drunk a fair amount of punch, and I was ready for bed. As I was saying goodnight to my hosts and wishing everyone a merry Christmas, Julie slipped her arm into mine and said she'd be going home too.

When we were outside, I said, 'Where do you live, Julie?'

'At Wolfsburn,' she said. 'Right at the top of the hill.'

'There's a cold wind,' I said. 'And although your dress is beautiful, it doesn't look very warm. Here, you'd better wear my overcoat. I've plenty of protection.'

She did not protest, and allowed me to slip my overcoat over her shoulders. Then we started out on the walk home. But I did not have to escort her all the way. At about the spot where we had met, she said, 'There's a shortcut from here. I'll just scramble up the hillside.'

'Do you know it well?' I asked. 'It's a very narrow path.'

'Oh, I know every stone on the path. I use it all the time. And besides, it's a really bright night.'

'Well, keep the coat on,' I said. 'I can collect it tomorrow.'

She hesitated for a moment, then smiled and nodded. She then disappeared up the hill, and I went home alone.

The next day I walked up to Wolfsburn. I crossed a little brook, from which the house had probably got its name, and entered an open iron gate. But of the house itself, little remained. Just a roofless ruin, a pile of stones, a shattered chimney, a few Doric pillars where a veranda had once stood.

Had Julie played a joke on me? Or had I found the wrong house?

I walked around the hill, to the mission house where the Taylors lived and asked old Mrs Taylor if she knew a girl called Julie.

'No, I don't think so,' she said. 'Where does she live?'

'At Wolfsburn, I was told. But the house is just a ruin.'

'Nobody has lived at Wolfsburn for over forty years. The Mackinnons lived there. One of the old families who settled here. But when their girl died . . .' She stopped and gave me a queer look. 'I think her name was Julie . . . Anyway, when she died, they sold the house and went away. No one ever lived in it again, and it fell into decay. But it couldn't be the same Julie you're looking for. She died of consumption—there wasn't much you could do about it in those days. Her grave is in the cemetery, just down the road.'

I thanked Mrs Taylor and walked slowly down the road, to the cemetery; not really wanting to know any more, but propelled forward almost against my will.

It was a small cemetery under the deodars. You could see the eternal snows of the Himalayas standing out against the pristine blue of the sky. Here lay the bones of forgotten empire builders—soldiers, merchants, adventurers, their wives and children. It did not take me long to find Julie's grave. It had a simple headstone with her name clearly outlined on it:

Julie Mackinnon
1923–39
'With us one moment,
Taken the next,
Gone to her Maker,
Gone to her rest.'

And although many monsoons had swept across the cemetery, wearing down the stones, they had not touched this little tombstone.

I was turning to leave, when I got a glimpse of something familiar behind the headstone. I walked round to where it lay.

Neatly folded on the grass was my overcoat.

No thank-you note. But something soft and invisible brushed against my cheek, and I knew someone was trying to thank me.

A TRAVELLER'S TALE

Gopalpur-on-sea!

A name to conjure with . . . and as a boy I'd heard it mentioned, by my father and others, and described as a quaint little seaside resort with a small port on the Orissa coast. The years passed, and I went from boyhood to manhood and eventually old age (is seventy-six old age? I wouldn't know), and still it was only a place I'd heard about and dreamt about, but never visited.

Until last month, when I was a guest of KiiT International School in Bhubaneswar, and someone asked me where I'd like to go, and I said, 'Is Gopalpur very far?'

And off I went, along a palm-fringed highway, through busy little market-towns with names Rhamba and Humma, past the enormous Chilika Lake, which opens into the sea through paddy fields and keora plantations, and finally on to Gopalpur's Beach Road, with the sun glinting like gold on the great waves of the ocean, and the fishermen counting their catch, and the children sprinting into the sea, tumbling about in the shallows.

But the seafront wore a neglected look. The hotels were empty, the cafes deserted. A cheeky crow greeted me with a disconsolate caw from its perch on a weathered old wall. Some of the buildings were recent, but around us there were also the shells of older buildings that had fallen into ruin. And no one was going to preserve these relics of a colonial past. A small house called 'Brighton Villa' still survived.

But away from the seafront a tree-lined road took us past some well-maintained bungalows, a school, an old cemetery, and finally a PWD rest house, where we were to spend the night.

It was growing dark when we arrived, and in the twilight I could just make out the shapes of the trees that surround the old bungalow—a hoary old banyan, a jackfruit and several mango trees. The light from the bungalow's veranda fell on some oleander bushes. A hawk moth landed on my shirt front and appeared reluctant to leave. I took it between my fingers and deposited it on the oleander bush.

It was almost midnight when I went to bed. The rest-house staff—the caretaker and the gardener—went to some trouble to arrange a meal, but it was a long time coming. The gardener told me the house had once been the residence of an Englishman who had left the country at the time of Independence, some sixty or more years ago. Some changes had been carried out, but the basic structure remained—high ceilinged rooms with skylights, a long veranda and enormous bathrooms. The bathroom was so large you could have held a party in it. But there was just one potty and a basin. You could sit on the potty and meditate, fixing your thoughts (or absence of thought) on the distant basin.

I closed all doors and windows, switched off all lights (I find it impossible to sleep with a light on) and went to bed.

It was a comfortable bed, and I soon fell asleep. Only to be awakened by a light tapping on the window near my bed.

Probably a branch of the oleander bush, I thought, and fell asleep again. But there was more tapping, louder this time, and then I was fully awake.

I sat up in bed and drew aside the curtains.

There was a face at the window.

In the half-light from the veranda, I could not make out the features, but it was definitely a human face.

Obviously, someone wanted to come in, the caretaker perhaps, or the chowkidar. But then, why not knock on the door? Perhaps he had. The door was at the other end of the room, and I may not have heard the knocking.

I am not in the habit of opening my doors to strangers in the night, but somehow I did not feel threatened or uneasy, so I got up, unlatched the door and opened it for my midnight visitor.

Standing on the threshold was an imposing figure.

A tall, dark man, turbaned, and dressed all in white. He wore some sort of uniform—the kind worn by those immaculate doormen at five-star hotels; but a rare sight in Gopalpur-on-sea.

'What is it you want?' I asked. 'Are you staying here?'

He did not reply but looked past me, possibly *through* me, and then walked silently into the room. I stood there, bewildered and awestruck, as he strode across to my bed, smoothed out the sheets and patted down my pillow. He then walked over to the next room and came back with a glass and a jug of water, which he placed on the bedside table. As if that were not enough, he picked up my day clothes, folded them neatly and placed them on a vacant chair. Then, just as unobtrusively, and without so much as a glance in my direction, he left the room and walked out into the night.

Early next morning, as the sun came up like thunder over the Bay of Bengal, I went down to the sea again, picking my way over the puddles of human excreta that decorated parts of the beach. Well, you can't have everything. The world might be more beautiful without the human presence; but then, who would appreciate it?

Back at the rest house for breakfast, I was reminded of my visitor from the previous night.

'Who was the tall gentleman who came to my room last night?' I asked. 'He looked like a butler. Smartly dressed, very dignified.'

The caretaker and the gardener exchanged meaningful glances.

'You tell him,' said the caretaker to his companion.

'It must have been Hazoor Ali,' said the gardener, nodding. 'He was the orderly, the personal servant of Mr Robbins, the port commissioner—the Englishman who lived here.'

'But that was sixty years ago,' I said. 'They must all be dead.'

'Yes, all are dead, sir. But sometimes the ghost of Hazoor Ali appears, especially if one of our guests reminds him of his old master. He was quite devoted to him, sir. In fact, he received this bungalow as a parting gift when Mr Robbins left the country. But unable to maintain it, he sold it to the government and returned to his home in Cuttack. He died many years ago, but revisits this place sometimes. Do not feel alarmed, sir. He means no harm. And he does not appear to everyone—you are the lucky one this year! I have but seen him twice. Once, when I took service here twenty years ago, and then, last year, the night before the cyclone. He came to warn us, I think. Went to every door and window and made sure they were secured. Never said a word. Just vanished into the night.'

'And it's time for me to vanish by day,' I said, getting my things ready. I had to be in Bhubaneswar by late afternoon, to board the plane for Delhi. I was sorry it had been such a short stay. I would have liked to spend a few days in Gopalpur, wandering about its backwaters, old roads, mango groves, fishing villages, sandy inlets . . . Another time perhaps. In this life, if I am so lucky. Or the next, if I am luckier still.

At the airport in Bhubaneswar, the security asked me for my photo identity. 'Driving licence, PAN card, passport? Anything with your picture on it will do, since you have an e-ticket,' he explained.

I do not have a driving licence and have never felt the need to carry my PAN card with me. Luckily, I always carry my passport on my travels. I looked for it in my little travel bag and then in my suitcase, but couldn't find it. I was feeling awkward, fumbling in all my pockets, when another senior officer came to my rescue. 'It's all right. Let him in. I know Mr Ruskin Bond,' he called out, and beckoned me inside. I thanked him and hurried into the check-in area.

All the time in the flight, I was trying to recollect where I might have kept my passport. Possibly tucked away somewhere inside the suitcase, I thought. Now that my baggage was sealed at the airport, I decided to look for it when I reached home.

A day later, I was back in my home in the hills, tired after a long road journey from Delhi. I like travelling by road—there is so much to see—but the ever increasing volume of traffic turns it into an obstacle race most of the time. To add to my woes, my passport was still missing. I looked for it everywhere—my suitcase, travel bag, in all my pockets.

I gave up the search. Either I had dropped it somewhere, or I had left it in Gopalpur. I decided to ring up and check with the rest-house staff the next day.

It was a frosty night, bitingly cold, so I went to bed early, well covered with a razai and blanket. Only two nights previously I had been sleeping under a fan!

It was a windy night, the windows were rattling; and the old tin roof was groaning, a loose sheet flapping about and making a frightful din.

I slept only fitfully.

When the wind abated, I heard someone knocking on my front door.

'Who's there?' I called, but there was no answer.

The knocking continued, insistent, growing louder all the time.

'Who's there?' I called, but there was no answer.

The knocking continued, insistent, growing louder all the time.

'Who's there? *Kaun hai*?' I called again.

Only that knocking.

Someone in distress, I thought. I'd better see who it is. I got up shivering, and walked barefoot to the front door. Opened it slowly, opened it wider. Someone stepped out of the shadows.

Hazoor Ali salaamed, entered the room, and as in Gopalpur, he walked silently into the room. It was lying in disarray because of my frantic search for my passport. He arranged the room, removed my garments from my travel bag, folded them and placed them neatly upon the cupboard shelves. Then, he did a salaam again and waited at the door.

Strange, I thought. If he did the entire room, why did he not set the travel bag in its right place? Why did he leave it lying on the floor? Possibly he didn't know where to keep it; he left the last bit of work for me. I picked up the bag to place it on the top shelf. And there, from its front pocket, my passport fell out, on to the floor.

I turned to look at Hazoor Ali, but he had already walked out into the cold darkness.

THE SKULL

I am not normally bothered by skeletons and old bones—
they are, after all, just the chalky remains of the long dead—
so that, when my nephew, Anil, came back from medical
college with a well-preserved skull, it was no cause for alarm.
He was a second-year student, at times a bit of a prankster.

'I hope you didn't take it without permission,' I said,
taking the skull in my hands and admiring its symmetry, but
without philosophizing upon it like Hamlet.

'Oh, the college is full of them,' said Anil. 'I just borrowed
it for the vacation.' He placed it on the mantelpiece, among
some of the awards and mementos (cheap brassware mostly)
that had accumulated over the years, and I must say it livened
up the shelf a little.

Anil had placed the skull at one end of the mantelpiece,
and there it stood until we'd had our dinner. He settled down
with a book, while I poured myself a small glass of cognac,
before settling into an easy chair with a notebook on my knee.
It was midsummer, and the window was open, so that we
could hear the crickets singing in the oak trees. My cottage
was on the outskirts of Mussoorie, surrounded by Himalayan
oak and maple.

I had been making some notes for an article on wild
flowers. When I had finished my notes and cognac, I looked
up and noticed that the skull now stood at the centre of the
mantelpiece.

'Did you move the skull?' I asked.

'No,' said Anil, looking up. 'I placed it at the end of the shelf'

'Well, it's now in the middle. How did it get there?'

'You must have moved it yourself, without noticing. That was a stiff cognac you drank, Uncle.'

I let it pass; it did not seem important.

* * *

People often dropped in to see me. School teachers, visitors to the hill station, students, other writers, neighbours. During that week I had a number of visitors, and, of course, everyone noticed the skull on the mantelpiece. Some were intrigued, and wanted to know whose skull it was. One or two lady teachers were frightened by it. A fellow writer thought it was in bad taste, displaying human remains in my sitting room. One visitor offered to buy it.

I would have gladly sold the wretched thing, but it belonged to Anil, and he intended taking it back to Meerut. But when the time came to leave, he forgot about the skull, his mind, no doubt, taken up with other matters—such as the daily phone calls he received from a girl student in Delhi. After seeing him off at the bus stop, I came home to find that the skull was still occupying pride of place on the mantelpiece.

I ignored it for a few days, and the skull didn't seem to mind that. It was receiving plenty of attention from visitors during the day.

But it was beginning to get on my nerves. Every evening when I sat down to enjoy a whisky or a cognac, I would feel its empty eye sockets staring at me. And on one occasion, when I tried to change its position, my hand got caught in its jawbone, and it was with some difficulty that I withdrew it.

Getting fed up of its presence, I decided to lock the thing away where it couldn't be seen.

There was a wall cupboard in the room, where I kept my manuscripts, notebooks and writing materials, and there was plenty of room there for the skull. So I shifted it to the cupboard and made sure the door was locked.

That evening I enjoyed my drink without being watched by that remnant of a human head. The crickets were singing, a nightjar was calling, and a zephyr of a wind moved swiftly through the trees. I finished my article and went to bed in a happy frame of mind.

In the middle of the night, I woke to a loud rattling sound. At first I thought it was a loose door latch or an insecure drainpipe; then I realized the noise was coming from the wall cupboard. A rat, perhaps? But no, as soon as I opened the cupboard door, out popped the skull, landing near my feet and bouncing away, right across the dining room.

For the sake of peace and quiet, I returned it to the mantelpiece. If a skull could smile, it would probably have done so. I went back to my bed and slept like a baby. It takes more than a dancing skull to keep me from enjoying a good night's sleep.

Next morning, I got to work, making up a parcel. Normally I hate making parcels; they usually fall apart. But for once I took pleasure in making a parcel. I wrapped the skull in a plastic bag, then placed it in a strong cardboard box, wrapped this in brown parcel paper, used a liberal amount of Sellotape, and addressed the package to Dr Anil at his medical college. Then I walked into town and handed it over to the registration clerk at the post office.

Rubbing my hands with satisfaction, I treated myself to fish and chips and an ice cream, before setting out on the walk down the hill to my cottage.

How did the skull get out of that parcel? I shall never know. Perhaps a nosy postal clerk had opened it to check the contents. I hope he got the fright of his life.

Anyway, I was about halfway down the steep path that leads to one of our famous schools, when I heard something rattling down the slope behind me. At first I thought it was an empty tin, but then I recognized my boon companion, that wretched skull, embellished with bits of wrapping paper and Sellotape, bouncing down the hill, towards me. I broke into a run, making a dash for the cottage door. But it was there before me, grinning up at me from a pot full of flowering petunias.

So back it went to its favourite place on the mantelpiece. And there it remained for several weeks.

* * *

The school's playing field was situated just above the path to the cottage, and during the football season, I could hear the boys kicking a football around.

One day a football escaped from the field and came bouncing down the hillside, landing in a flower bed. The match got over and no one bothered to come down to retrieve the ball. But it gave me an idea. I removed the bladder, stuffed the skull into the leather interior and tied it up firmly. Then I had the football delivered to the school's games master with my compliments.

Nothing happened for a couple of days. There was no shortage of footballs. Then, in the middle of the game against St. George's College, a ball went out of the grounds and a spare one was required.

The replacement didn't bounce quite as well as the previous one, and it was inclined to spin around a lot and take off in directions opposite to those intended. Also, it squeaked

whenever it received a kick, and sometimes those squeals sounded a bit like screams of protest. The goalkeeper at either end found the ball difficult to hold—it did its best to elude their grasp. And more goals were scored by accident rather than design. Finally, this eccentric ball was kicked out of play and was replaced by another.

What happened to old footballs? I expect they finally fall apart and end up in a dustbin.

In this case, the football found a new owner, for the sports master was a kind man who gave away old bats, balls and other worn-out stuff to the poor children of the locality. A boy from a village near Rajpur was the recipient of the battered football, and he and his friends carried it away with a cheer, kicking it all the way down the steep path, making so much noise that they did not hear the groans of protest that issued from the battered old football.

Well, weeks passed, months passed, without the skull making a reappearance. But then something strange began to happen. I found myself missing that troublesome skull!

It had, after all, been company of a sort for a lonely writer living on his own on the edge of the forest. And when you have lived with someone for a very long time, then no matter how much you may quarrel or get on each other's nerves, a bond is formed, and the strength of that bond can only be known when it is broken.

The skull had been sharing my life for over a year, and now that it was gone, seemingly forever, my life seemed rather empty.

So I began searching for the skull. I inquired amongst the children down in Rajpur; but they had long since lost the football. I made a round of all the junk shops in Dehradun, without any luck. There were lots of old footballs lying around, but not the one I wanted. And no, they didn't buy or sell human skulls.

Young Anil, the doctor, paid me a brief visit and found me looking depressed.

'What's the trouble?' he asked. 'You look as though you have just lost a friend.'

'I have, indeed,' I said. 'I miss that skull you gave me. It was company of a sort.'

'Well, I'll get you another. No shortage of skulls in my college.'

'No, I don't want another. I want the same skull. It had a personality of its own.' Anil looked at me as though he thought I was going off my rocker. And perhaps I was.

And then one day, as I was walking down a busy street in neighbouring Saharanpur, I noticed a fortune teller plying his trade on the pavement. I don't believe in fortune telling, but everyone has to make a living, and telling fortunes seems to me a harmless way of doing it. And then I noticed that he had a skull beside him, and that he would consult it before handing his customer a slip of paper with words on it. It looked a bit like my skull, but I couldn't be sure. All the kicking and manhandling it had received had possibly altered its appearance.

But anyway, I gave the fortune teller some money and asked him for a prediction. He chanted something, then extracted a slip of paper from beneath the skull and handed it to me with a flourish.

I read the words printed neatly on paper.

'*Ullu ka pattha* (Son of an owl)!' went the message, followed by '*Gaddhe ka baccha* (Child of a donkey)!' It was definitely my skull! Only an old friend could abuse me like that.

So I pleaded and haggled with the fortune teller, paid him a hundred rupees for the skull and carried it home in triumph.

And there it is today, decorating my mantelpiece, a little the worse for wear, and with a silly grin on its skeletal face. To improve its looks I have placed an old cricket cap on its head.

Sometimes we don't value our friends until we lose them.

A BLOODTHIRSTY VAMPIRE CAT

Hours later, another bus delivered the boys to a dimly lit bus stand on the outskirts of Chakrata. It was almost deserted except for the few arrivals who disappeared into the surrounding gloom. A few lights twinkled on the hillside. Tall deodars loomed out of the darkness. Dogs howled.

'Why are the dogs howling?' asked Rusty.

'They howl when there are evil spirits around,' replied Popat. 'That's what my grandmother told me.'

'She's probably right,' mused Rusty. 'Dogs bark at people and at other animals. They howl at what they can't see or hear.'

'This is the end of the earth,' said Pitamber, looking about in dismay.

'Only the end of the road,' said Rusty.

'And where do we eat?' asked Pitamber. 'It's only nine o'clock but everything is shut.'

'My father gave me an address,' said Popat. The boys hopefully set out in search of it but were told that it was on the far side of the town. There was no hotel. Then someone told them to try the old forest rest house. No one went there any more—not since a new one had been built for visiting forest officials.

So off they trudged, helped, to some extent, by a half-moon that occasionally appeared between the scurrying clouds. Popat had wisely brought along a pencil torch but they used it sparingly, knowing the battery wouldn't last too long.

Down below, in the thick of the forest, they saw a faint light—the glow of a lantern standing on a veranda wall.

'That must be it!' exclaimed Rusty.

They stumbled down a narrow path which led to the veranda steps. The rest of the building was in darkness, seemingly unoccupied. In the distance, a dog howled.

'This place is full of howling dogs,' said Popat. 'I say we go back to Dehra in the morning, after I've seen my father's clients.'

'Let's do some howling too,' suggested Rusty. 'There must be a chowkidar somewhere.'

So they began shouting, 'Chowkidar! Chowkidar!' and presently, another lamp appeared from the rear of the building, moving towards them very slowly, almost as though there was no one behind it. But gradually a figure manifested itself, and the man who held the lamp raised it so that he could see their faces, at the same time revealing his own.

It was the face of a one-eyed man. A scar ran down one side of his face. It was hard to tell his age—he may have been fifty, he may have been seventy. He wore a funny-looking hat; it looked like a bowler hat, something left behind by a British official.

'What do you want?' he asked suspiciously, for he was wary of high-spirited students.

'Shelter,' said Rusty.

'Food,' said Pitamber at the same time.

'Do you have any money?'

'Er—a little,' said Popat cautiously.

'Very little,' added Rusty, who didn't like the man's attitude.

'All right, you can come in. There's a spare room. Wait until I put on the lights.'

Finally, there was light everywhere. The front room had a large dining table in the middle. Then there was a bedroom with two double beds and a huge, cavernous bathroom with a basin at one end and a potty at the other. And there was a kitchen—which looked empty.

Pitamber made a quick inspection of the kitchen and discovered some stale chapatis.

'You could play table tennis with these,' he said.

'Probably made in Emperor Ashoka's time,' added Rusty.

But the chowkidar promised to rustle up some food and the boys made themselves at home. Pitamber did some exercises. Popat studied a small notebook and made some calculations. Rusty stared out of the window into the night. The light of the half-moon played upon the trees and bushes opposite the clearing. A large black cat emerged from the shrubbery and crept towards the rest house; the kitchen light gave promise of a meal.

The caretaker-cum-cook-cum-chowkidar came up with quite a decent meal—a vegetable curry, dal and lots of hot chapatis—and watched them as they tore into the food.

'And where is your journey taking you?' he asked. 'It is not yet the trekking season.'

'To the top of the Witch Mountain,' said Rusty.

'Ah, but no one goes there any more. There are only a few ruins there now. No one lives on the mountain, although many years ago it was the home of kings and queens. Sometimes people wander up there and don't come back. They go looking for a treasure that doesn't exist.'

'We'll come back,' said Popat. 'We have to! I have an exam to take!'

'And there's a wrestling tournament coming up,' said Pitamber. 'Five thousand rupees if I win all my bouts.'

They went to bed early. Pitamber took over one of the beds, while Rusty and Popat shared the other. They had barely settled down when they felt a slight tremor. Then all the lights went out.

'Did you feel that?' asked Popat.

'The bed shook a little,' said Rusty. 'Could it be an earthquake?'

'Maybe it's just Pitamber moving around,' Popat chortled.

But soon there was another tremor, more distinct than the first, and all the windowpanes began rattling. Rusty and Popat jumped out of bed.

'It is an earthquake!' exclaimed Rusty. But there were no further tremors, and presently, Rusty and Popat returned to their bed. Pitamber was still fast asleep; the mild earthquake had not bothered him. They lived in a region that was prone to such tremors and there were tales of an extinct volcano that sometimes showed signs of activity.

Rusty slept soundly till about midnight, when he was woken by someone or something scratching on the windowpanes. The window was locked, and at first he assumed that the scratching was caused by the cat he had seen earlier that evening. But the sound continued, *scratch scratch scratch*, and finally, Rusty got up and reached for the light switch. Only to find that all the lights had gone, probably because of the earthquake. So he went to the window and peered through the glass. At first he saw nothing. Then he made out the shape of the black cat he had seen earlier. Feeling sorry for it, he opened the window and it darted into the room, purring softly.

Rusty returned to his bed and the cat followed him, curling up near his feet. He was not particularly fond of cats and his first impulse was to push it off the bed. And then he thought, it's probably used to sleeping in this room. I'll let it be, as long as it doesn't trouble Popat or start chasing rats! But all it did was come a little closer, advancing from Rusty's feet to his knees, and purr loudly, as though quite satisfied with the situation.

Lulled by the purring of the cat, Rusty fell asleep. He slept for a couple of hours, before he was awakened by a feeling of wetness under his right armpit. His vest was wet and something was sucking away at his flesh.

It was with a feeling of horror that he discovered that the cat was now stretched out beside him and that it was licking away at his bleeding armpit with a certain amount of relish. And the purring was louder than ever.

A bloodsucking cat!

Rusty sat up on the bed, flung the cat away from him, sent Popat rolling to the floor and made a dash for the light switch.

As the lights came on, Rusty saw the cat standing at the foot of the bed, tail erect and hair on end. It looked very angry.

And then, for the space of five seconds at the most, its appearance changed. Its face was that of a human—a girl's face, beautiful but anguished, with full, red lips that were drenched with blood . . .

The moment passed and it was a cat's face again. It let out a weird mewing, leapt on to the windowsill and disappeared through the open window.

Quickly, Rusty shut the window and examined himself in the mirror. His vest was soaked with blood. For over an hour the cat had been licking and sucking at his fragile skin, wearing it away until the blood oozed out.

'What happened to you, Rusty?' asked Popat, now wide awake. 'Why are you bleeding?' He followed Rusty into the bathroom and helped him wash the blood away.

'It was a cat,' exclaimed Rusty, 'or a vampire!' But he had not been bitten. There were no teeth marks, no scratches. The tongue and the constant licking had done the damage.

Popat found a roll of cotton wool in his backpack, and used some of it to stop the trickle of blood from Rusty's armpit. Then he dabbed boric powder on the wound and made a rough bandage out of a couple of large handkerchiefs.

'I didn't know you were a doctor,' said Rusty, appreciating Popat's efforts.

'I'll get some proper bandages when I'm in the bazaar,' said Popat, 'but how did the cat get in?'

'It was all part of a dream, I think,' said Rusty. A nice dream at first, but then it had changed—and dreams and reality were all mixed up now.

Rusty returned to his bed, uncertain about what he had seen. How had the cat's face changed just for a few moments? Had it been a vision, a dream or the embodiment of a spirit?

'A bad dream,' professed Popat. 'Let's just go home tomorrow.'

'If you like,' agreed Rusty.

* * *

After many adventures on the Magic Mountain, the boys returned to Dehra and their everyday activities. Rusty wonders if their strange experience was all a dream, but when he examines himself in the mirror, he finds the imprint of the cat's tongue under his armpit. And it's still there today!

Note: This is an excerpt from *Rusty and the Magic Mountain*, Puffin Books India, 2015.

SOME HILL-STATION GHOSTS

Simla has its phantom rickshaw and Lansdowne, its
headless horseman. Mussoorie has its woman in white.
Late at night, she can be seen sitting on the parapet
wall on the winding road up to the hill station. Don't stop to
offer her a lift. She will fix you with the evil eye and ruin your
holiday.

The Mussoorie taxi drivers and other locals call her Bhoot
Aunty. Everyone has seen her at some time or the other. To give
her a lift is to court disaster. Many accidents have been attributed
to her baleful presence. And when people pick themselves up
from the road (or are picked up by concerned citizens), Bhoot
Aunty is nowhere to be seen, although survivors swear that she
was in the car with them.

Ganesh Saili, Abha and I were coming back from
Dehradun late one night, when we saw this woman in
white sitting on the parapet by the side of the road. As our
headlights fell on her, she turned her face away. Ganesh,
being a thorough gentleman, slowed down and offered her
a lift. She turned towards us then, and smiled a wicked
smile. She seemed quite attractive, except that her canines
protruded slightly in vampire fashion.

'Don't stop!' screamed Abha. 'Don't even look at her! It's
Bhoot Aunty!'

Ganesh pressed down on the accelerator and sped past
her. Next day we heard that a tourist's car had gone off the

road and the occupants had been severely injured. The accident took place shortly after they had stopped to pick up a woman in white who wanted a lift. But she was not among the injured.

* * *

Miss Ripley-Bean, an old English lady who was my neighbour when I lived near Wynberg-Allen School, told me that her family was haunted by a malignant phantom head that always appeared before the death of one of her relatives.

She said her brother saw this apparition the night before her mother died, and both she and her sister saw it before the death of their father. The sister slept in the same room. They were both awakened one night by a curious noise in the cupboard facing their beds. One of them began getting out of bed to see if their cat was in the room, when the cupboard door suddenly opened and a luminous head appeared. It was covered with matted hair and appeared to be in an advanced stage of decomposition. Its fleshless mouth grinned at the terrified sisters. And then as they crossed themselves, it vanished.

The next day, they learnt that their father, who was in Lucknow, had died suddenly, at about the same time that they had seen the death's head.

* * *

Everyone likes to hear stories about haunted houses; even sceptics will listen to a ghost story, while casting doubts on its veracity.

Rudyard Kipling wrote a number of memorable ghost stories set in India—'The Return of Imray', 'The Phantom

Rickshaw', 'The Mark of the Beast', 'At the End of the Passage'—his favourite milieu being the haunted dak bungalow. But it was only after his return to England that he found himself actually having to live in a haunted house. He writes about it in his autobiography, *Something of Myself*:

The spring of '96 saw us in Torquay, where we found a house for our heads that seemed almost too good to be true. It was large and bright, with big rooms each and all open to the sun, the ground embellished with great trees and the warm land dipping southerly to the clean sea under the Mary Church cliffs. It had been inhabited for thirty years by three old maids.

The revelation came in the shape of a growing depression which enveloped us both—a gathering blackness of mind and the sorrow of the heart, that each put down to the new, soft climate and, without telling the other, fought against for long weeks. It was the Feng-shui—the spirit of the house itself—that darkened the sunshine and fell upon us every time we entered, checking the very words on our lips . . . We paid forfeit and fled. More than thirty years later we returned down the steep little road to that house, and found, quite unchanged, the same brooding spirit of deep despondency within the rooms.

Again, thirty years later, he returned to this house in his short story, 'The House Surgeon,' in which two sisters cannot come to terms with the suicide of a third sister, and brood upon the tragedy day and night, until their thoughts saturate every room of the house.

Many years ago, I had a similar experience in a house in Dehradun, in which an elderly English couple had died from neglect and starvation. In 1947, when many European residents were leaving the town and emigrating to the UK, this poverty-stricken old couple, sick and friendless, had been forgotten. Too ill to go out for food and medicine, they had died in their beds, where they were discovered several days later by the landlord's munshi.

The house stood empty for several years. No one wanted to live in it. As a young man, I would sometimes roam about the neglected grounds or explore the cold, bare rooms, now stripped of furniture, doorless and windowless, and I would be assailed by a feeling of deep gloom and depression. Of course, I knew what had happened there, and that may have contributed to the effect the place had on me. But when I took a friend, Jai Shankar, through the house, he told me he felt quite sick with apprehension and fear. 'Ruskin, why have you brought me to this awful house?' he said. 'I'm sure it's haunted.' And only then did I tell him about the tragedy that had taken place within its walls.

Today, the house is used as a government office. No one lives in it at night except for a Gurkha chowkidar, a man of strong nerves, who sleeps in the back veranda. The atmosphere of the place doesn't bother him, but he does hear strange sounds in the night. 'Like someone crawling about on the floor above,' he tells me. 'And someone groaning. These old houses are noisy places . . .'

* * *

A morgue is not a noisy place, as a rule. And for a morgue attendant, corpses are silent companions.

Old Mr Jacob, who lives just behind the cottage, was once a morgue attendant for the local mission hospital. In those days, it was situated at Sunny Bank, about a hundred metres up the hill from here. One of the outhouses served as the morgue; Mr Jacob begs me not to identify it.

He tells me of a terrifying experience he went through when he was doing night duty at the morgue.

'The body of a young man was found floating in the Aglar river, behind Landour, and was brought to the morgue while I was on night duty. It was placed on the table and covered with a sheet.

'I was quite accustomed to seeing corpses of various kinds and did not mind sharing the same room with them, even after dark. On this occasion, a friend had promised to join me, and to pass the time, I strolled around the room, whistling a popular tune. I think it was "Danny Boy", if I remember right. My friend was a long time coming, and I soon got tired of whistling and sat down on the bench beside the table. The night was very still, and I began to feel uneasy. My thoughts went to the boy who had drowned, and I wondered what he had been like when he was alive. Dead bodies are so impersonal . . .

'The morgue had no electricity, just a kerosene lamp, and after some time I noticed that the flame was very low. As I was about to turn it up, it suddenly went out. I lit the lamp again, after extending the wick. I returned to the bench, but I had not been sitting there for long when the lamp again went out, and something moved very softly and quietly past me.

'I felt quite sick and faint, and could hear my heart pounding away. The strength had gone out of my legs, otherwise I would have fled from the room. I felt quite weak and helpless, unable even to call out . . .

'Presently the footsteps came nearer and nearer. Something cold and icy touched one of my hands and felt its way up towards my neck and throat. It was behind me, then it was before me. Then it was *over* me. I was in the arms of the corpse!

'I must have fainted, because when I woke up, I was on the floor and my friend was trying to revive me. The corpse was back on the table.'

'It may have been a nightmare,' I suggested 'Or you allowed your imagination to run riot.'

'No,' said Mr Jacobs. 'There were wet, slimy marks on my clothes. And the feet of the corpse matched the wet footprints on the floor.'

After this experience, Mr Jacobs refused to do any more night duty at the morgue.

* * *

A Chakrata Haunting

From Herbertpur, near Paonta, you can go up to Kalsi, and then up the hill road to Chakrata.

Chakrata is in a security zone, most of it off limits to tourists, which is one reason why it has remained unchanged in the 150 years of its existence. This small town's population of 1500 is the same today as it was in 1947—probably the only town in India that hasn't shown a population increase.

Courtesy a government official, I was fortunate enough to be able to stay in the forest rest house on the outskirts of the town. This is a new building, the old rest house—a little way downhill—having fallen into disuse. The chowkidar told me the old rest house was haunted, and that this was the real reason for its having been abandoned. I was a bit sceptical about this, and asked him what kind of haunting took place in it. He told me that he had himself gone through a frightening experience in the old house, when he had gone there to light a fire for some forest officers who were expected that night. After lighting the fire, he had looked round and seen a large animal, like a wild cat, sitting on the wooden floor and gazing into the fire. 'I called out to it, thinking that it was someone's pet. The creature turned and looked full at me with *eyes that were human*, and a face which was the *face of an ugly woman*! The creature snarled at me, and the snarl became an angry howl. Then it vanished!'

'And what did you do?' I asked.

'I vanished too,' said the chowkidar. 'I haven't been down to that house again.'

I did not volunteer to sleep in the old house but made myself comfortable in the new one, where I hoped I would not be troubled by any phantom. However, a large rat kept me company, gnawing away at the woodwork of a chest of drawers. Whenever I switched on the light it would be silent, but as soon as the light was off, it would start gnawing away again.

This reminded me of a story old Miss Kellner (of my Dehra childhood) told me, of a young man who was desperately in love with a girl who did not care for him. One day, when he was following her in the street, she turned on him and, pointing to a rat which some boys had just killed, said, 'I'd as soon marry that rat as marry you.' He took her cruel words so much to heart that he pined away and died. After his death, the girl was haunted at night by a rat and occasionally she would be bitten. When the family decided to emigrate, they travelled down to Bombay in order to embark on a ship sailing for London. The ship had just left the quay, when shouts and screams were heard from the pier. The crowd scattered, and a huge rat with fiery eyes ran down to the end of the quay. It sat there, screaming with rage, then jumped into the water and disappeared. After that (according to Miss Kellner), the girl was not haunted again.

* * *

Old dak bungalows and forest rest houses have a reputation for being haunted. And most hill stations have their resident ghosts—and ghostwriters! But I will not extend this catalogue of ghostly hauntings and visitations, as I do not want to discourage tourists from visiting Landour and Mussoorie. In some countries, ghosts are an added attraction for tourists. Britain boasts of hundreds of haunted castles and stately homes, and visitors to Romania seek out Transylvania and Dracula's castle. So do we promote Bhoot Aunty as a tourist attraction? Only if she reforms and stops sending vehicles off those hairpin bends that lead to Mussoorie.

Read more in Puffin by Ruskin Bond

Rusty and the Magic Mountain

'Adventure is for the adventurous'

Rusty and his friends, Pitamber and Popat, find adventure in no small measure when they set out to climb a mysterious mountain steeped in legend and superstition. On the way they shelter in a haunted rest house, encounter a tiger and experience a hilarious mule ride which takes them to the palace of a mad rani.

Ruskin Bond returns with a brand new Rusty adventure after more than a decade. A rollicking tale of humour and enchantment, *Rusty and the Magic Mountain* will win the much-loved character of Rusty a whole new band of followers.

Read more in Puffin by Ruskin Bond

Panther's Moon and Other Stories

'He heard something scratching at the door, and the hair on his head felt tight and prickly. It was like a cat scratching, only louder. The door creaked a little whenever it felt the impact of the paw . . . "It's the panther," Bisnu muttered under his breath, sitting up on the hard floor.'

Ten unforgettable tales of fascinating human encounters with animals and birds—of a man-eater that terrorizes an entire village; a strange and wonderful trust that develops between a fierce leopard and a boy; revengeful monkeys who never forgive a woman who grows dahlias; a crow who genuinely thinks human beings are stupid, and many others, creating a world in which men and wild creatures struggle to survive despite each other—a world where, in the end, one is not quite sure which side one is on.

Ruskin Bond, the author of the popular *Angry River* and *Flames in the Forest*, once again gives a marvellous collection of stories that enchant, amuse and delight.

Read more in Puffin by Ruskin Bond

Escape from Java and Other Tales of Danger

Join intrepid heroes and dauntless heroines in their quest for survival against earthquakes, fire, floods and bombs!

Live life on the edge with five stories of danger and adventure. Flee with Romi as he rides his cycle straight into the river to escape a fearsome forest fire; listen in to Ruth's hair-raising story of escape from rioting sepoys during the uprising of 1857; read about the author's miraculous flight from Java as Japanese planes bombard the city; witness the havoc wreaked by the deadliest earthquake ever in Rakesh's town, Shillong; and watch Sita combat a fatal flood that threatens to engulf her.

Thrilling plots, daring protagonists, explosive exploits—this book has it all! Written in Ruskin Bond's inimitable style, with doses of humour and excitement, these extraordinary stories are simply unputdownable.